"It was my choice. And for what it's worth, it was the second-best decision I ever made."

Now it was Ava who hesitated. "What was the first?"

"Telling you how I really felt. Laying all my cards on the table. I never had to look back with regret. I never had to wonder what-if."

Her hackles rose in self-defense. "You assume that I have?"

"I never said that. I speak only for myself."

The conversation was getting a little too intimate for comfort. Ava felt a sense of relief at having survived their first encounter, but now she searched for a subtle excuse to go her own way even though a part of her wanted to just stand there and stare at him forever.

She opened her mouth, but before she could utter a sound, a scream pierced the night, jangling her nerves and freezing her to the spot. For a moment, she stood in horrified silence, unable to breathe, unable to move until a second scream propelled her straight into Dylan Burkhart's arms.

WHISPERING SPRINGS

AMANDA STEVENS

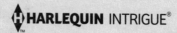

Recycling programs
for this product may
not exist in your area.

ISBN-13: 978-1-335-63891-5

Whispering Springs

Printed in U.S.A.

Amanda Stevens is an award-winning author of over fifty novels, including the modern gothic series The Graveyard Queen. Her books have been described as eerie and atmospheric, "a new take on the classic ghost story." Born and raised in the rural South, she now resides in Houston, Texas, where she enjoys binge-watching, bike riding and the occasional margarita.

Books by Amanda Stevens

Harlequin Intrigue

Pine Lake
Whispering Springs

MIRA Books

The Graveyard Queen

The Restorer
The Kingdom
The Prophet
The Visitor
The Sinner
The Awakening

Visit the Author Profile page at Harlequin.com.

CAST OF CHARACTERS

Ava North—Trapped by raging floodwaters and stalked by a ruthless killer, assistant DA Ava North teams up with a man who mysteriously disappeared from her life ten years ago.

Dylan Burkhart—A former army ranger turned security consultant, he's been hired to protect Tony Redding from a ruthless business rival, but the killer stalking Whispering Springs has a more personal motivation.

Blair Redding—She's invited her closest college friends to Whispering Springs for a long-overdue reunion. But the gathering is shattered when a killer issues a deadly invitation: *Play the game.*

Tony Redding—He's been receiving threatening phone calls from someone he claims is a business rival. But is he the victim or instigator of a nefarious scheme?

Celeste Matthews—A vivacious redhead with a mean streak. What is her real motive for coming to the reunion...and what is her real relationship with Tony Redding?

Jane Sandoval—She's carried a chip on her shoulder since Lily Callen's tragic suicide on graduation weekend. Has she come to the reunion to exact her pound of flesh?

Lily Callen—Ten years ago, guilt over Lily's suicide drove Ava North from Dylan Burkhart's arms. Now Lily's ghost haunts their reunion.

Noah Pickett—Whispering Springs had been in his family for generations. Now he is an employee. Does he harbor a secret resentment toward the new owner?

Sarah Rainey—An employee of Whispering Springs, she went out one evening to walk the trails and was never heard from again.

Chapter One

The bored driver waited for her at baggage claim, placard in hand as he scanned the harried travelers. There was her name in big bold lettering: Ava North.

She was almost embarrassed to wave him over. It wasn't like she'd been traveling for hours or needed assistance getting from point A to point B. The flight from Houston to San Antonio had taken all of fifty minutes, less time than the commute from her apartment to the airport.

Ava could have easily headed west on I-10 in her own vehicle, but Blair Redding, the former college classmate who had put together this ill-advised gathering, had insisted on arranging all the transportation. No doubt with the intent of making it harder to leave before the week was up. Ava wouldn't be at all surprised if she and the other guests were asked to relinquish their cell phones once they arrived at the destination. Blair had always been that much of a control freak.

Steeling herself for the coming days, Ava put up her hand to attract the young man's attention. She didn't like vacations in general and reunions in particular. Spending time at a remote ranch with the people she'd left behind years ago was a version of hell she would have preferred to avoid, yet here she was. An uncharacteristic outburst in district court had jeopardized not only what should have been a slam-dunk case but also her five-year career as an assistant DA. The judge had threatened to hold her in contempt, and her superior had promised a suspension if she didn't make herself scarce for a few days.

"You're exhausted," he'd said, not without sympathy. "The caseload we get in this office wears us all down eventually, and you do yourself no favors with the hours you keep. How long has it been since you put in for a personal day, let alone a real vacation? Go," he'd insisted when she tried to formulate a passable defense. "Get out of my sight before I'm forced to do something drastic."

Ava had dragged herself home, where she intended to drink and fume for the rest of the day. But idleness, her mother always said, was Ava's worst enemy, followed closely by the unholy trinity of overreaction, righteous indignation and self-destruction. No matter how appealing the thought of a good wallow, Ava knew a week of brooding in her apartment would lead nowhere good. So she'd dug the invitation out of the trash and RSVP'd at the last minute. Then she'd packed a bag and headed for the airport that same afternoon without allowing herself time to reconsider.

The man with the placard gave her a perfunctory smile as he picked up her suitcase. "This is it? Just the one?"

"That's it. I'm Ava, by the way."

"Noah Pickett."

"Have the others arrived yet, Noah?"

"Two flew in over the weekend. They came with a lot of baggage," he felt compelled to add.

Ava wondered if she was to take his observation literally or figuratively.

"Do you remember their names?"

"Jane got in on Saturday. The redhead came on Sunday. I don't remember her name, but I remember her," he said with a grin.

No man alive ever forgot Celeste Matthews. "What about Blair? I assume she's already at the ranch."

"Since last week," he confirmed with a nod. "Her husband is arriving today."

So they were all there, Ava thought with a shiver. With the exception of Lily, of course. Lily Callen had been the group's first tragedy, a horrifying suicide on graduation weekend that had left everyone stunned. The days following her jump from a hotel rooftop had passed in a nightmarish blur of police interrogations and funeral preparations. Afterward the friends had parted in a flurry of tearful goodbyes and silent recriminations. Ava had fled to the isolation of her family's beach house for the summer. Blair had gotten married. Celeste had backpacked through Europe with a guy she barely knew before settling down in New Orleans with another. Jane had moved to California.

And Dylan Burkhart, the love of Ava's life, had disappeared off the face of the earth.

Funny how his desertion still niggled at

times, mostly when she was already feeling blue or vulnerable. No reason why it should, of course. After all, she was the one who had ended their relationship. She was the one who had sent him away. Told him in no uncertain terms that it was over and she didn't want to see him anymore. She'd just never considered that he would take her at her word.

No matter. Some things weren't meant to be, and Ava had no regrets. She was happy enough with her chosen path, but her time in the DA's office had changed her. Not that her physical appearance was so different. Same brown hair. Same green eyes. But she'd become hardened and world-weary. A cynic though she'd once been a romantic.

Such was the life of a prosecutor, she thought with an inward shrug.

She wondered how Blair had coerced the others into coming, especially Jane. She'd been the first to lose touch. Ava hadn't seen or heard from Jane Sandoval since the day she'd driven her to the airport. That strange goodbye had lingered with Ava all summer long, but then law school had consumed her time and attention and she'd eventually moved on, too.

Over the years, she'd heard from the others sporadically. Celeste still lived in New Orleans and Blair was in Austin. For a while, the three of them had made an effort to get together, but their visits had been awkward and unpleasant. The events surrounding Lily's death had eroded their friendship, and Ava was only too happy to put those days behind her. She rarely thought of any of the women anymore. Even Dylan was little more than a passing memory. Or so she told herself.

"Have you ever been to Whispering Springs?" The driver gave her a sidelong glance as he stored her bag in the back of the SUV.

"A few times in college. A group of us used to go out there to rock climb. Spooky place."

"You're a climber?"

"Not me, no. I have a thing about heights. I like to hike, though, so long as the trail doesn't get too vertical."

"You'll find plenty of easy trails around the ranch," he assured her. "How long has it been since you were there?"

"At least ten years."

"You won't recognize it now. The owners have completely restored the property. I thought they were crazy when they first came in with a boatload of cash and a scheme to turn a run-down old ranch into a retreat, but the place has been booked solid since they opened seven years ago."

"I just remember how isolated it was. And the springs really did seem to whisper, especially at night." An unexpected chill seeped in as Ava thought back to those weekend excursions. Had their first trip to Whispering Springs been the start of her feelings for Dylan? Or had she been secretly in love with him for years, hiding it from herself and the others because he was taken?

"It's a natural phenomenon," Noah was saying.

"The springs?"

"The whispering. It has something to do with the rock formations."

"Oh, I see. No ghosts, then," she teased.

"I didn't say that." A shadow flickered across his face as he waited for her to climb in the back seat. Then he closed the door and went around to slide behind the wheel.

"What did you mean by that?" Ava asked curiously as he started the car and merged with the airport traffic.

He shrugged. "Nothing important. Just shooting the breeze."

"Really? Because I get the feeling I said something that disturbed you." She caught his eye in the rearview mirror. "Did I?"

"Your mention of ghosts reminded me of an old story. An urban legend, I guess you'd call it. I hadn't thought about it in a long time."

"I like urban legends," Ava said. "Why don't you entertain me while we drive?" She settled back against the seat and tried to relax, but as their gazes connected again in the mirror, she felt another inexplicable shiver along her spine.

"There was a girl once, a college kid who worked at the ranch when it first opened. One evening after her shift, she went out to walk the trails and never came back. The cops were called in and a search party formed, but they didn't find so much as a footprint. It was like she vanished into thin air."

"Wait a minute," Ava said with a frown. "I think I remember reading something about that disappearance. It happened while I was still in law school. The police suspected her boyfriend, but they could never find her body."

"That was just an easy explanation to avoid a lot of bad publicity for the new retreat."

"And I thought I was cynical," Ava muttered. "What do you think happened to her?"

"Beats me, but no one who knew her bought that story. Her boyfriend had an airtight alibi. The police couldn't pin it on him no matter how hard they tried."

"Doesn't mean he didn't have something to do with it," Ava said.

"He wasn't even in the area. And if she ran away like some folks thought, she would have told her friends or at least left a note. A person doesn't just walk out the door and disappear off the face of the earth."

"It could happen." Ava thought about Dylan. "Did you know her?"

"Before my time," he said, but with an edge in his voice that made Ava wonder. "Anyway, to circle back to the urban legend part, when the wind blows down through the canyon, people claim they can hear her scream."

"Have you heard her?"

"Me? No. But I don't wander too far off the beaten path after dark. The terrain is deceptively rugged even for those of us who grew up around there. Don't go out alone," he advised. "Travel in a group or hire a guide. If you prefer solitude, then stick to the trails close to the house."

"Thanks. I'll keep that in mind."

They both fell silent after that. Ava leaned her head against the back of the seat and watched the passing scenery. Traffic thinned as they left the city, and the road wound through the countryside like a twisted gray ribbon. After a while, the fenced meadows gave way to a breathtaking vista of ridges and valleys in earthy hues of slate, ocher and moss.

Ava felt unaccountably anxious. She wanted to blame her disquiet on Noah's story or even the mess she'd left behind in Houston. Deep down, she knew better. She hadn't thought through this trip. Until now, she hadn't allowed herself to dwell on the consequences of facing her former friends and all their old demons.

She closed her eyes and tried to block out the foreboding. The road noise lulled her and the next thing she knew, the car had pulled to a stop. She sat up abruptly. "Are we there?"

"Ten miles out," Noah told her. "I need to gas up. Hope you don't mind."

"No, of course not. Where are we, exactly?"

"Lawton. It's the nearest town to the ranch. Not much to see, but you're welcome to get out and stretch your legs if you want. I'll come find you when I'm done."

"Thanks. I wouldn't mind a stroll." Ava got out of the car and stretched, then set out in the direction she vaguely remembered as downtown. She passed a couple of eateries, a cluttered antiques shop, the post office, a hardware store and a handful of other businesses lined up along the main drag. There was no picturesque town square, no quaint gazebo or clock tower to attract passersby. The place had seen better days, but there was charm to the dusty windows and peeling paint. A stubborn resistance to the march of time that Ava found comforting.

At the edge of town, the cracked sidewalk gave way to a dirt footpath that disappeared into a cedar thicket. The sun beat down warm on her shoulders as she drank in the fresh air. The sky was very blue and mostly cloudless, but a shadow on the horizon warned of rain.

She stood for another moment enjoying the woodsy spice of the evergreens and the distant gurgle of a creek fed by underground springs. Then she turned to retrace her steps to the gas station. She hadn't encountered a single soul on her short excursion, although she'd glimpsed a handful of patrons and shop-keepers through plate glass windows. Enough to know she was hardly alone, and yet the oddest sensation of isolation beset her. She wanted to hurry back as fast as she could to the car, but instead she halted and scanned her surroundings, searching for the reason for her sudden unease.

He stood on the opposite side of the street, sheltered beneath an old tin awning so that at first Ava could detect little more than a tall, lean silhouette. She told herself not to stare, *move on, nothing to see here.*

But she remained rooted to the spot, her gaze fixed on the stranger. As her eyes adjusted to the shade, she could make out his clothing and features. He had on jeans, boots and a plaid shirt common to the area, but Ava didn't think him a local. There was something about the way he carried himself, about the slight tilt of his head that struck a chord. A memory.

It couldn't be, she thought in near panic. Not after all this time. She was seeing things. A mirage, a dream, a trick of light and shadow. Why, after all these years, would Dylan Burkhart turn up in Lawton, Texas, of all places?

She resisted the urge to cross the street for a closer look and the even greater desire to flee in the opposite direction. Instead, she skimmed her surroundings yet again, testing her perception. She wasn't dreaming or imagining things. She was fully cognizant.

But when she glanced across the street, the silhouette had vanished.

DYLAN BURKHART STEPPED BACK into the shop, moving quickly to the window, where he fastened his gaze on the woman across the street. For a moment, he wondered if she meant to come look for him. He could have sworn she took a step toward the curb. Then she turned with a shrug and moved on down the street.

He watched her walk away with a mixture of relief and regret, doused with icy shock. She wasn't supposed to be here. He'd known there was a chance she'd show up, of course, but from everything he'd been able to ascertain, Ava North rarely took time off from her job. She'd become a workaholic, a tireless prosecutor who never used vacation or sick days and who rarely ventured beyond the triangle of her apartment, the courthouse and her office. And yet here she was.

She'd changed since their final parting. She could still turn heads, but there was a cynical twist in her smile that hadn't been there in the old days. Not that he'd taken all that in from a quick observation across the street. In the year since he'd relocated to Houston, he'd seen her twice before—once in a restaurant and once from the shadows across the street from her apartment. The first time had been by chance, the second by design. He hadn't set out to look her up. Told himself when he accepted the position in Houston that he would let sleeping dogs lie.

But then he'd started seeing mentions of her in the paper, along with an occasional photograph. She was a rising star in the DA's office. No surprise there. She'd always been smart and driven, but the woman who stared up at him from the pages of the *Chronicle* seemed so different from the young crusader he'd known in college. She still had that wild mane of brown hair, but tamed for court in a loose bun. Her green eyes still sparkled, but now with a deadly determination.

He hadn't approached her either time. He'd observed her from afar until he'd sated his curiosity, and then he'd gone about his business of starting a new job and finding a place to live. And he'd made certain they never traveled in the same circles. Until now.

"Something I can help you with?" the clerk asked from behind the counter.

"Just browsing," Dylan replied absently, his gaze still on the street.

"Holler if you need anything."

"I will, thanks."

He waited until she was out of sight and then exited the store with a nod to the curious shopkeeper. He moved down the street, keeping to the shady side until he caught a glimpse of her. She was getting into a white SUV with the Whispering Springs logo on the side. Leaning his back against a building, he watched the vehicle pull out of the gas station and onto the road. After the dust cloud settled, he walked back to his own car, following at a discreet distance, although it didn't much matter if he was spotted. He'd already checked into his room at the ranch, and his client would make certain the others bought his cover.

As he navigated the winding road, he rolled down his window, allowing the scents and sounds of the rugged countryside to settle over him. It had taken a long time after three tours of duty in the Middle East to silence the noise of war in his head. When he first came back, he'd had no plan beyond finding a little peace and quiet. With his undergrad degree and service record, he'd had no shortage of opportunities, but for a while, he'd used the money left to him by his grandmother to hibernate.

For nearly a year, he'd done nothing but camp and hike and read. Then dinner with an army buddy had brought him to Houston and to an informal interview with Ezra Blackthorn, the founder and CEO of the Blackthorn Agency, a global security firm. Dylan had turned down the offer of overseas assignments despite the generous bonus incentives. He'd had his fill of foreign chaos. The domestic side of the agency was more to his liking, in particular surveillance where he could blend into the woodwork.

He'd settled quietly into his new life in Houston. He completed his assignments, kept to himself and that was that. Then one day he'd walked into Ezra Blackthorn's office and been confronted by his past. Blair Redding had heard about his work at the agency through a friend of a friend. She was in need of protection for her CEO husband who had received a series of threats in the wake of a rumored merger.

Tony Redding had refused to take the threats seriously, but for Blair, a line had been crossed when someone had broken into their home and scribbled a troubling message across the bathroom mirror. She wanted to hire the Blackthorn Agency and Dylan in particular to provide covert protection during their upcoming stay at Whispering Springs.

Dylan had received a list of guests and staff, and he'd noted with relief the absence of Ava's name. Would he have backed out of the assignment if he'd known she would come? He couldn't answer that question and it didn't matter anyway, because he was here now and he had a job to do.

Pulling off the main road, he drove through the arched entrance to the ranch and slowed his vehicle as he took stock of his surroundings. Nestled against a verdant hillside of wildflowers and rushing creeks, Whispering

Springs was bordered on one side by a line of rugged live oaks, cedars and Texas pinions and on the other side by a natural barrier of arroyos and canyons carved from the walls of limestone bluffs.

The white SUV was parked on the circular drive when Dylan arrived at the house. He pulled to the rear and grabbed his backpack before heading up into the hills. According to Blair, her husband was due to arrive at the ranch around dinnertime that evening. As far as Tony Redding and the others knew, Dylan was just another invited guest. But instead of mingling or relaxing, he'd spent the last few days getting the lay of the land. He'd explored the ranch house and outbuildings, the walking trails, the creek beds, the ravines and outcroppings—anywhere a perpetrator might hide.

Leaving the trail, he continued to climb until he had a panoramic view of the area. He lifted his binoculars, trailing his gaze along the tree line, peering into the evergreen thicket before zeroing in on the ranch house, a sprawling limestone structure with rough-hewn beams and outside arbors. No one was about. The chairs and gliders placed strategically around the property for sunrise and sunset viewings were all empty and the porches sat forlornly deserted. It would be dinnertime soon. Maybe everyone was inside getting ready for the evening meal.

As he turned to store his gear, something flashed in his peripheral vision. He turned back, scouring the valley with a naked eye before once again lifting his binoculars. He didn't see anything at first, but he'd long ago learned the value of patience.

After a moment, the flash came again from one of the upstairs windows. He made note of the location even though the glare seemed nothing more than sunlight bouncing off glass. But the longer he lingered, the more convinced he became that someone stood just beyond his line of sight, watching him back through binoculars.

Ava LEANED AGAINST the balcony rail of her second-floor bedroom and surveyed the breathtaking scenery. The sun was just setting, gilding the jagged ridges that rose beyond the tree line. A breeze ruffled her hair, and she absently tucked back the wayward strands as her gaze lit on a lone hiker making his way toward the ranch. He was still some distance away, too far to make out his features, but his confident gait seemed familiar.

Recognition mingled with unease as Ava stepped back into the shadows. As he drew closer, she could see that he was tall and lean with close-cropped brown hair. She even imagined a slight auburn tinge to his five o'clock shadow. He had on sunglasses, but she knew behind those dark lenses his eyes were a piercing blue.

A memory came to her now of those electric eyes peering down at her intently as she held fast to her determination.

"Please don't look at me that way. We both know it's over."

"It's not over for me, Ava. I still love you. I still want us to be together. Nothing's changed."

"Everything's changed! When we're together, all I can think about—"

"Don't. You're hurt and confused and you feel guilty. But what happened wasn't our fault. We didn't do anything wrong."

"Then why are we still keeping secrets?"

He was crossing the grounds now, and for a moment, Ava had the strongest urge to step out of the shadows and call down to him.

I loved you, too, Dylan. I was wrong about us. It doesn't matter now, of course, but I thought you should know.

She held her ground and in the next instant, he paused as if sensing her scrutiny. His right hand dropped to his side as he turned casually to observe the path behind him. Then he scanned the woods, the canyon and finally the house. His gaze slowly lifted. Ava was certain he couldn't spot her in the shadows, and yet she could have sworn their eyes connected a split second before he crossed the grounds and entered through one of the side doors.

Her head fell back against the wall as she let out a shaky breath. Crazy to feel so stunned by the mere glimpse of an old boyfriend, but the sight of Dylan Burkhart had caught her completely off guard. He was the last person she'd expected to see here. Ava didn't really care about the how or the why of his presence at the ranch. Her only concern was her reaction to him.

She took several calming breaths, trying to quiet her racing pulse. This wasn't her. She was not that woman. She didn't live in the past or carry torches. She didn't dwell on what might have been. She'd moved on.

Forged ahead. There'd been no one really serious since Dylan, but that had nothing to do with unrequited love and everything to do with ambition. She simply had no time for anything more than a casual relationship. No strings, no commitment, no expectations.

Her reaction meant nothing. She could handle this. Already she felt steadier. Soon she would get dressed and go downstairs for dinner, where she would spend a pleasant evening reminiscing with old friends.

But first, she'd have a long soak and a good stiff drink.

Chapter Two

The great room was empty when Ava came downstairs a little while later. She milled about for a bit, studying the William B. Travis portrait over the fireplace and the framed photographs on either side before moving through the French doors to the terrace. The sun had set by this time and the sky over the treetops had deepened to lavender. She could smell mountain laurel on the breeze and a hint of rain in the distance.

The feeling of disquiet that had descended earlier came back as she took in the isolation of her surroundings. Except for the muted clatter of china and silverware coming from the dining room, she might have been alone. But then she sensed another presence a split second before she spotted a silhouette in the deepest shadows of the patio. She wanted to turn away from his relentless gaze, seek refuge inside the lit great room. Instead, she took a step toward him.

"Dylan?"

"Hello, Ava."

Her hand fluttered to her chest. "My goodness. It really is you."

"You seem surprised to see me. No one told you I'd be here?"

His voice was rich and deep and very unsettling. Ava shivered as the breeze blew across the terrace. "I came at the last minute. I haven't spoken with the others yet."

She still couldn't see him clearly but she very much wanted to. She wanted to know if the flesh-and-blood man could hold a candle to her memory. Not a fair comparison, she acknowledged. Time had marched on. She wouldn't like to be held to the same standard.

As if reading her mind, he stepped out of the shadows. Her hand was still at her chest. She could feel the pounding of her heart through her sweater and forced her hand to her side.

He was still peering at her through the

twilight. "You don't have a problem with my being here, do you?"

"Why would I have a problem? You were always a part of this group. You belong here as much as anyone." She sounded fine, but her smile felt brittle. She drew a breath and tried to relax. "But I didn't realize you'd kept in touch with the others."

"I didn't. Blair and I ran into each other through a mutual acquaintance. She invited me to the reunion. I had nothing else planned so here I am."

"Here you are," Ava echoed faintly.

He returned her cautious smile. "It's good to see you. You're looking well."

"Am I? That's kind of you to say, but I'm feeling a bit of a mess these days." She touched her ponytail, wishing she'd taken a little more care with her appearance. Wishing she'd worn the navy sheath rather than the black pants and sweater. "You, though…" She trailed off, taking in the fitted charcoal slacks and jacket. She sighed and dispensed with discretion. "You look fantastic. I kind of hate you right now."

He laughed, a soft, intimate sound that

wrapped around her like an embrace. "Why are you feeling a mess?"

"Oh, work. Life." She shrugged. "The usual."

His gaze deepened as he searched her face. "Can't be more than a temporary setback. I hear impressive things about you."

She stared back at him. "You do? Oh, that's right. You said you ran into Blair. She's biased, you know."

"I doubt she needs to be in your case. She tells me you're an attorney." He leaned a shoulder against a post as he observed her in the waning light. "It's nice to know you followed through with your dream of law school. I can't remember you ever wanting to do anything else."

"Yes, although I didn't go into practice with my dad. I work for the DA's office in Houston."

"Challenging work, I imagine."

"It can be." She shoved her hands into her pockets as she gazed at him across the terrace. There was a surreal quality to their casual conversation after a decadelong separation. Ava tried to decide if the meeting was easier or harder than she had imagined it would be. "You have me at a disadvantage. I haven't heard anything about you. In all these years…not one word." Her voice took on an accusatory edge despite her best efforts.

His voice held no such edge. "I thought that's what you wanted."

"It was. But I can still be curious, can't I? What have you been up to since college? Are you married, single…? What do you do for a living?" The questions tumbled out before she could stop them.

There was a slight hesitation before he answered. "I'm still figuring out what I want to do. I've been at loose ends since I left the army."

She went completely still. "You were in the service?"

"You didn't know? I enlisted the day after graduation."

Ava felt as if the wind had been knocked from her lungs. "I had no idea. Why didn't you tell me?"

"You know why."

"The others…?"

"I didn't tell anyone. It seemed best that way. After you left, there was nothing keeping me in Austin. My grandmother was dead. Most of our friends had scattered." He canted his head, still watching her. "I needed a purpose and I found one."

"The army," she murmured. "For how long?"

"Eight years."

"Were you overseas?"

"Afghanistan for a time."

She closed her eyes. "I wish I'd known. I should have known."

"Why?"

"It doesn't seem right, you over there in that nightmare and the rest of us here getting on with our lives."

"It was my choice. And for what it's worth, it was the second-best decision I ever made."

Now it was Ava who hesitated. "What was the first?"

"Telling you how I really felt. Laying all my cards on the table. I never had to look back with regret. I never had to wonder 'what if.'"

Her hackles rose in self-defense. "You assume that I have?"

"I never said that. I speak only for myself."

The conversation was getting a little too intimate for comfort. Ava felt a sense of relief at having survived their first encounter, but now she searched for a subtle excuse to go her own way, even though a part of her wanted to just stand there and stare at him forever.

She opened her mouth, but before she could utter a sound, a scream pierced the night, jangling her nerves and freezing her to the spot. For a moment, she stood in horrified silence, unable to breathe, unable to move until a second scream propelled her straight into Dylan Burkhart's arms.

DYLAN'S FIRST INSTINCT was to pull her tightly to him, protect her from whatever danger lurked on the property, but that wasn't a good idea for so many reasons. Too many years had passed and he had a job to do. He held her for only a moment before sliding his hands to her shoulders, subtly keeping her at bay.

"Did you hear that?" she asked on a breath. "Sounded like it came from directly above us."

"Hold on." He shifted his position, putting his body between her and the shadowy grounds as he moved out from under the terrace to scan the second-story bedrooms. Only one of the windows was lit against nightfall. He saw a movement in the room and then, a second later, a female figure appeared in the balcony doorway.

"Blair?" he called up to her softly.

She rushed out on the balcony, clutching a white robe to her chest. "Dylan?"

"Are you okay?"

"I'm not hurt, but you'd better get up here." Her hushed voice quivered with excitement. Or was that panic?

"What's wrong?"

"Just come up, okay?"

Ava caught his arm, her eyes wary and anxious as he moved back under the lattice cover. "What's going on?"

"That's what I'm trying to find out." He gently untangled his arm. "Wait here while I go have a look."

"What? No! Are you crazy? I'm not waiting out here alone in the dark."

"Then come inside." He took her hand, pulling her toward the French doors. "I'll be back down as soon as I can."

"If Blair's in trouble, I should go up there and help her. Dylan, those screams—" She broke off. "Wait a minute. How is it you're still so calm? You don't even seem surprised. It's almost as if you—"

"As if I what? You heard her. She said she's fine. There's no cause for panic."

"You don't scream like that if you're fine."

"Then why are we standing here arguing?" he asked in exasperation.

"That's a very good point." She brushed past him to the doorway.

Dylan hesitated for only a moment before catching up with her and taking the lead. He bounded up the stairs two at a time, pausing on the landing to take stock. A crystal chandelier tinkled overhead in a draft. Farther down the hallway, a door clicked shut. He turned his ear to the sound, holding up his hand to silence Ava when she would have questioned his caution.

Blair had arranged to have the ranch exclusively for the reunion. The invitees had all been assigned rooms upstairs, leaving the detached cabins unoccupied. In the two days that Dylan had been there, he'd made a point to familiarize himself with all the staff members. A stranger wandering around the house or grounds should be easy to spot. He scoured the hallway now for any sign of an intruder or anything out of the ordinary. Except for that faint click of a door, nothing seemed amiss.

Blair's suite was just off the landing, and as Dylan started toward the door, she burst into the hallway, the hem of her silk robe floating behind her like a ghost.

"Dylan, thank God. You have to see this—" She halted abruptly when she spotted Ava. Her hand flew to her throat in alarm. "Ava! I didn't know you were here."

"I got in a little while ago." She moved around Dylan. "What's going on? We heard your screams. That was you, wasn't it?"

"Yes…"

"You scared us half to death," Ava said. "It sounded as if you were being murdered up here."

Blair seemed at a loss as her gaze darted to Dylan. "Murdered? No… I…"

"Take a breath," he said, "and tell us what happened." He kept his voice neutral, but his eyes warned her to proceed with caution.

She bit her lip and nodded. "I'm okay. I… it's nothing really. I feel completely stupid. I saw a scorpion in my bedroom."

"A scorpion?" Ava repeated in disbelief.

"On my bed." Blair clutched the lapels of her robe. "They're everywhere in the Hill Country so I shouldn't be surprised, I suppose. But you remember how deathly afraid of spiders I've always been. A scorpion is a million times worse."

Ava nodded. "I remember, all right. You nearly drove us into a ditch once when you saw a spider in your car."

Blair shuddered. "It was a very big spider."

"I can see you're upset," Ava said. "Why don't I call downstairs and have someone come up and take care of the problem?"

Dylan maneuvered around Blair to the door, blocking Ava's path into the suite. "I'll deal with the scorpion. You go downstairs and let everyone know that Blair is fine. We can't be the only ones who heard her scream."

"Yes, would you?" Blair managed a weak smile. "I'm too embarrassed to face anyone right now."

"There's no need to be embarrassed. I'm sure I would scream, too, if I found a scorpion in my bed." Ava addressed Blair, but she trained her gaze on Dylan. Unease niggled. He could almost hear the gears turning inside her head. The scorpion cover wasn't bad, but Ava North had never been anyone's fool.

"Thanks," Blair murmured.

Ava shrugged off her gratitude, but she had

a determined look on her face that Dylan remembered only too well. "Think nothing of it. I'll take care of everything. But are you sure you're okay? You still look a little pale. My room is just down the hall. Would you like to wait there while Dylan exterminates yours?"

"I'm fine now."

"If you say so." Her gaze on Dylan was direct and slightly challenging. "You've got everything under control up here?"

"Yes, no worries."

She nodded though she didn't look particularly convinced. "I'll see you both downstairs, then."

Dylan waited until she'd disappeared across the landing before turning back to Blair. "What happened?"

"It's better if I show you."

He followed her into the suite. A small entryway opened into a luxurious sitting area with buttery leather furniture, a limestone fireplace and a row of French doors that looked out on a wide balcony. Blair paused in the sitting room and pointed to a doorway through which Dylan could glimpse a bed and another set of French doors.

"In there."

The lamp on the nightstand cast a soft glow over the room. More light spilled in from the open bathroom door. Dylan quickly scanned the area, peering into shadowy corners and taking note of the night air drifting in through the open balcony doors. Like the sitting area, the room was both rustic and luxurious with a vaulted beam ceiling and plush rugs on a wide-plank floor. But it was the bed that drew Dylan's attention. Or rather, what had been placed on the covers.

Lying atop the opulent linens was a doll, the kind of expensive keepsake his grandmother had once collected and kept behind the locked glass doors of her curio cabinet. Only this one hadn't been so lovingly preserved. The porcelain arms and legs had been shattered and the neck grotesquely twisted so that the painted visage faced the doorway. Light glinted in the glass eyes, prickling Dylan's scalp as he moved into the room.

Behind him, Blair said breathlessly, "You see it, don't you?"

He glanced over his shoulder. "The doll?"

"It's not just a doll. It's an effigy. Notice the color of her hair, those eyes. The way she's been posed. You must see it." A note of hysteria rose in her voice. "Dylan, it's Lily. *Your* Lily."

Chapter Three

Dylan turned slowly to face her. "What did you say?"

Blair leaned back against the door frame. "Surely you can see it, too."

He whirled back to the bed, more shaken than he cared to admit. For a moment, he almost let her persuade him. There was something eerily familiar about the doll. Something perverted and sinister about the shattered limbs, the twisted neck and those open, staring eyes. He'd seen a lot of bad things in Afghanistan, dark things, but no amount of death and destruction could obliterate the image of Lily Callen's broken body after a twenty-story fall. He wondered if the others still had nightmares about that night.

About the lies that had been told and the secrets that had been kept.

"I don't blame you for being upset," he said. "But it's a reach to think the doll is an effigy of Lily."

"Is it? The blond hair, the blue eyes? The way she's been placed on the bed? You think all that's just a coincidence?" Something in her voice made Dylan glance over his shoulder again. She was clearly distraught, and yet her demeanor didn't seem quite right. He couldn't put his finger on it exactly, but unease stirred.

He turned back to the doll. "Of course it's not a coincidence. But Lily wasn't the only one with blond hair and blue eyes. That description fits you, too, Blair. I'd say if the doll is meant to represent anyone, it's you."

"Me? But what about the way the doll has been damaged?"

"As if she fell? Think about it for a minute. You and Tony are still avid climbers. There was a write-up about you in *Summit Magazine* not too long ago."

"How did you know about that article?" she asked in shock.

"It's my job to know."

That seemed to give her pause. "You think the person behind the phone calls and break-in did this?"

"Isn't that why you hired me? Because you were worried those threats would follow you here?" Dylan lifted his gaze from the doll, catching Blair's reflection in one of the windows. She wasn't looking at the bed. Her left hand was splayed in front of her and she seemed mesmerized by the sparkle of her diamond rings.

"Blair?"

Her hand dropped at once. "Yes?"

"You've told me everything, haven't you?"

"What do you mean?"

"You haven't received any other threats since you've been here?"

"No, everything's been fine."

Dylan moved around to the other side of the bed so that he could examine the shattered porcelain while keeping an eye on Blair. "Where were you before you found the doll?"

"I went down to the springs for a swim. I was gone for about two hours."

"No one else has a key to your room?"

"Just the staff."

"You didn't see anyone lurking in the hallway when you left? Anything out of the ordinary happen while you were out?"

"Not that I noticed. Dylan…" She took a reluctant step into the room, averting her gaze from the bed. "The other threats were more straightforward. The phone calls, the message left on the bathroom mirror. This is more nuanced. More diabolical somehow. If what you're saying is true…if the doll is meant to represent me, then Tony is no longer the target. I am."

"He could still be the ultimate objective. From everything you've told me, he's a ruthless negotiator. He doesn't give up or give in. Personal threats wouldn't faze him, but if his opponents believe you're his Achilles heel, they may think the best way to get to him is through you."

"If only they knew," she murmured.

"Meaning?"

"Nothing." Her head came up defiantly. "You're right. Tony doesn't give up or give in. No matter what. It may sound bizarre, but you've made me feel better. A stranger using me as leverage to gain the upper hand in a business deal is infinitely preferable to one of my oldest friends playing a malicious trick on me."

"Even so, you shouldn't take any of this lightly. This person has been watching you. He or she is familiar with your comings and goings, and they've managed to infiltrate your personal space not once, but twice. I'll have another look around the grounds and I'll talk to the staff, find out if any strangers have been spotted on the property. In the meantime, you should consider bringing in more security."

"You know I can't do that. I explained why in Ezra Blackthorn's office during our first meeting. Tony would never agree to protection. He'd see it as a sign of weakness. If I brought in a bunch of strangers, he'd catch on immediately and send you all away. Like it or not, you're our only defense, Dylan."

"I'll do whatever it takes to keep you safe, but I'm just one person and this is a large, isolated property. I can't be everywhere at once, so I'll say it again. Don't let your guard down and don't get careless."

"I understand."

He walked over to the French doors. "Were these open while you were gone?"

"Yes, the suite seemed a little stuffy. I wanted to air out the bedroom while I swam. We're on the second floor. I didn't think anyone could get in."

"Someone can always get in. It wouldn't take much skill or strength to scale the wall. Remind me again of the room arrangements?"

"Your room is across the hall, of course, and Ava is next to you. Celeste is at the end and Jane is across from her. There's an empty room between her room and this suite."

Dylan thought about the flash of light he'd seen earlier. He could have sworn someone had been watching him from a balcony doorway. "You're sure no one else is staying at the ranch besides staff? Not even in the cabins?"

"The last of the guests checked out over the weekend. I reserved the whole place for a week, so no one else should be arriving until Saturday. Except for Tony, of course. He's still due in tonight."

Dylan stepped out on the balcony. Twilight had deepened to nightfall and a few stars hung low on the horizon. He could see the glitter of the moon through the trees, but the leaves muted the illumination. He took out his cell phone and shone the beam across the floor and all along the rail, looking for any evidence left by the intruder. Then he straightened and gazed down the row of balconies. A curtain billowed next door.

He went back inside and latched the French doors. "You said the room next door is empty, correct?"

"Yes, why?"

"Wait here while I check something out. Don't let anyone in while I'm gone."

Blair shivered as her gaze darted to the bed. "What am I supposed to do with the doll?"

"Leave it. Don't touch anything. I'll take care of it when I get back."

He left the suite and strode down the hallway to the next room, pressing his ear to the door before knocking. He couldn't hear anything inside and the door was locked. He retraced his steps to Blair's suite. When she let him in, he went back out to the balcony.

Blair trailed after him. "Dylan? What are you doing?"

"Trying to figure out how someone got into your suite." He climbed on top of the railing and then hoisted himself up to the roof. From his vantage, he had an expansive view of the property. Light from the downstairs windows and patios cast an anemic glow over the grounds, but the woods beyond lay in deep shadow. The night was so quiet he could hear the ripple of leaves and the gurgle of a creek beyond the trees. To his right, the escarpment was a jagged silhouette against the navy sky.

He scanned the cliffs and probed all along the tree line. If anyone was out there, they were well hidden by the night.

Lifting his face to the sky, he closed his eyes for a moment as he tried to calm a festering worry. Something was wrong. He could sense discord all around him, could hear it in the eerie saw of the breeze that blew through the pinions. In the whisper of water over rocks from the springs. Somewhere on the ridge a coyote howled, followed by a series of yips and barks that lifted the hair at the back of his neck. They sensed it, too, he thought. He wasn't particularly insightful and definitely not clairvoyant, but he'd learned a long time ago not to second-guess his instincts.

The doll was a troublesome development. Nuanced and diabolical, Blair had said. Maybe they were both overthinking the situation, but Dylan couldn't shake the notion that more was going on beneath the surface. That the threats to Blair and Tony Redding might be nothing more than a clever ruse to lure Dylan and the others to Whispering Springs. But why?

A FEW MINUTES LATER, Dylan hurried along the edge of the roof and dropped down onto the next balcony.

Parting the billowing curtains, he stepped inside. The layout and furnishings were similar to those of his room. King-size bed facing a large armoire with a flat-screen TV and bar. Desk and chair situated in front of the French doors. Bathroom and closet just off the entry. A quick search through the armoire drawers and closet yielded nothing. The room appeared spotless, bed neatly made, fresh towels in the bathroom. It was possible the cleaning staff had left the balcony doors open by mistake, but he kept going back to the flash of light he'd seen from the escarpment.

He went out into the hallway, glancing both ways before returning a second time to Blair's suite. She answered his knock at once.

Before he could say anything, she leaned in to murmur, "Ava's here."

"Where?"

She pointed to the bedroom. "The door was open and she saw the doll. I couldn't stop her from going in."

He said nothing else as he moved out of the foyer and into the sitting room. Ava stood just beyond the bedroom doorway. She had her back to him, but she spun as soon as she heard him approach.

"Have you seen this?"

He took in her pale face and wide green eyes. "Yes, I've seen it."

"What do you make of it? What kind of sick joke is someone trying to pull here?"

Before he could answer, Blair came into the room, keeping her distance from the bed. "It's not a joke. It's a warning effigy."

Ava looked aghast. "A what?"

"Blair," Dylan cautioned.

She gave a helpless shrug. "What's the point of keeping her in the dark now? She's already seen the doll. Besides, maybe she can help keep an eye out."

"An eye out for what? For who?" Ava glanced from Blair to Dylan, her expression turning resolute and suspicious. "One of you had better start talking. And don't give me any nonsense about scorpions and spiders. Just tell me the straight-up truth. What's going on here?"

Dylan eyed Blair carefully. "It's your call."

She nodded before turning back to Ava. "Long story short, Tony is negotiating a merger for Redding Technologies. There's been a lot of opposition within both companies and from outside competitors. That's not unusual, but a couple of weeks ago, he started getting threatening phone calls at work. Then last week our house was broken into and someone left a message on the bathroom mirror."

"What was the message?"

"'Tell the truth.'"

"Tell the truth," Ava repeated with a pensive frown. "And you think that message has something to do with the merger?"

"Coming after the phone calls, it seems a logical conclusion," Dylan said.

Ava shot him a glance before turning back to the bed. She wore that look again, the one that told him she wasn't about to accept anything at face value.

"Do you know what truth they're talking about?" Ava asked.

"Tony doesn't talk much about his business deals," Blair hedged.

"Did you call the police?"

"No, because he doesn't take the threats seriously. He thinks the opposition is trying to rattle him. If we go to the police, they'll know they're getting to him. It would weaken his bargaining power."

"He's playing a risky game with your safety," Ava said as she moved around to the other side of the bed. She seemed to want to keep an eye on both of them while she examined the doll.

"I agree," Blair said. "It is risky. That's why I went behind my husband's back and hired Dylan. To Tony and everyone else, he's just another guest."

Ava's head came up. "What do you mean, you *hired* Dylan?"

He had remained silent for most of the exchange, preferring to let his client disclose as much or as little as she felt was warranted. But his gaze had remained on Ava, and now he saw a war of emotions on her face as she struggled to make sense of his deception.

"I work for a private security firm in Houston," he explained. "You may have heard of it—the Blackthorn Agency."

"Yes, I know of it." Her tone sounded stilted. "For how long?"

"A little over a year."

She shrugged, but her features hardened. "So much for being at loose ends."

I can explain, he wanted to tell her, but instead he allowed her to draw her own conclusions.

"Please don't say anything to the others," Blair pleaded. "I asked everyone here so that we could catch up and have a good time. Maybe even mend some fences. We were once like family."

"That was a long time ago," Ava said, her cool gaze brushing Dylan's before she looked away.

"And yet you're here." Blair's smile turned hopeful. "Call me sentimental, but I still miss what we had. I still miss *us*. I thought if we could all get together just one more time, we could somehow recapture the magic. Maybe that's just wishful thinking. Even so, I don't want to cast a pall over our reunion."

"I don't like any of this," Ava said. "I think

you should go to the police regardless of what Tony says. It's dangerous and irresponsible to do otherwise. I'll keep quiet for now, but if anything else happens, all bets are off." Her gaze dropped to the bed. "What are you going to do with this thing?"

Dylan moved around beside her. "I'll handle everything in here. Why don't you take Blair into the other room and fix her a drink? She still looks a little shaken."

Ava nodded. "Good idea. Maybe I'll fix one for myself while I'm at it."

Chapter Four

A little while later, Dylan answered the door of his room to Ava. She looked calm and collected, but there was something about her demeanor that put him on notice.

"Can I come in for a minute?"

He stepped back to allow her inside. "What's up?"

She strode into the room and turned with a glare. "How about we start with the doll? You don't really think it was put in Blair's bed because of some business deal, do you?"

Dylan took a moment before he responded, surprised at how hard he had to work to remain dispassionate. He didn't think he would be so affected by Ava's presence, but his chest tightened uncomfortably as he followed her into the room. She stood with her back to the balcony doors, arms at her sides, head slightly lifted. Dressed all in black, she looked ethereal and mysterious, a dangerous temptress with lamplight shimmering in her hair and something indefinable gleaming in her green eyes. The bombardment of memories was almost a physical pain as Dylan leaned a hip against the dresser and folded his arms.

"You have a different opinion, I take it."

Despite his measured tone, she gave him a withering assessment. "The shattered limbs? The twisted neck? And here we are together again at Whispering Springs after ten years of estrangement. You can't tell me this is all one big coincidence. Someone is messing with us."

"You weren't even supposed to be here," he reminded her.

"That's beside the point."

"You also conveniently disregard the other incidents. The break-in and phone calls happened weeks before the reunion. If you look at it as all of a piece, the doll fits a pattern."

Doubt flickered across her face. "But why a doll? More specifically, why a smashed doll?"

"This place isn't just known for its springs. Don't you remember why we started coming out here in the first place? Tony and Blair wanted to climb Bishop's Rock."

"So did you. Even Jane was gung ho at first, but then she stayed behind to keep me company because she knew how terrified I was of heights."

"Do you really think that's why she stayed behind?"

"Don't you?"

Dylan shrugged. "Jane has always been a hard one to figure out."

"Yes, she always did march to her own drum," Ava agreed as she turned to the window. She grew reflective. "Do you remember the last time we all came out here? We didn't know it then, but that trip was the beginning of the end for us."

Not true, Dylan thought. His breakup with Lily had been the first fracture in the once tight group.

Lily Callen had been a part of Dylan's life since childhood. They'd remained devoted all through high school and most of college until he'd finally admitted to his growing feelings for someone else. Their split had seemed amicable at first. Lily had even seemed relieved. It was time they both spread their wings, she'd said. But in the ensuing weeks, she'd grown increasingly moody and withdrawn. Then had come a series of disjointed, bordering on paranoid phone calls, followed by a final text message that had driven a stake through the heart of his fledgling relationship with Ava.

I told you I was in trouble. Why didn't you help me?

Ava watched him carefully as if trying to intercept his innermost thoughts. "You had a bad fall that weekend. The image of you tumbling down the side of Bishop's Rock still gives me nightmares."

Dylan smiled. "I managed to walk away in one piece."

"Thankfully."

They were still ignoring the ghost in the room. Neither seemed willing to speak Lily's name aloud, as if the mere mention could somehow breathe life into their old guilt.

Dylan said into the strained pause, "My point is, Blair and Tony are still avid climbers. It's common knowledge in their circle."

"You think someone is threatening Blair

with a fall? I don't know, Dylan. Even if we accept that premise, there's no way you can deny that doll's resemblance to Lily."

So there it was. The name hovered in the room like an old dream, and the knot in Dylan's chest turned into a different kind of pain. "The doll looks just as much like Blair."

"Maybe. But I still have a hard time believing this is about a business deal. It feels too personal." Her gaze turned cool and assessing. Whatever feelings Lily's name had evoked now lay hidden beneath Ava's lawyerly facade. "I can't help wondering if there's something you're still not telling me."

"Even if that were true, I'm not at liberty to discuss my client or her situation. You know that better than anyone."

"Yes, but as Blair pointed out, how am I to help you keep an eye on things if you leave me in the dark?"

Dylan straightened from the dresser, anxious to bring the conversation to an end. He remembered only too well Ava's persistence. No good could come from a prolonged confrontation. "You don't need to keep an eye out. That's my job."

"And now it's also mine. I can't unsee that

doll, and I can't go blithely about my business knowing what I know."

"You could try."

She gave him another look. "I have a question for you. You don't have to answer if you feel it violates your ethics."

"Go on."

"Are you sure *you* know the whole story?"

She'd surprised him. "Meaning?"

"You don't find it even a little strange that Tony Redding refuses to call the cops when his house is broken into?"

"Blair explained his reasoning."

"Yes, she did. But she couldn't explain the message that was left on the bathroom mirror, could she? 'Tell the truth.' What truth?"

Dylan said nothing.

She scowled at his silence. "Was a photograph taken of the mirror? What was used to write the message?"

"Ava."

His admonition merely emboldened her. "I can always go ask Blair."

He sighed. "The message was scribbled in lipstick."

"Blair's?"

"Apparently."

"The tube was left behind?"

"Yes."

"Cursive or printed?"

He paused. "Printed."

"*Was* a photograph taken?"

"Yes, but I would need Blair's permission to show it to you."

Ava nodded absently. "How did the perpetrator enter the residence?"

"Through an unlocked patio door."

"The alarm wasn't tripped?"

"They live in a gated community with round-the-clock security guards, so they weren't in the habit of setting the system."

"That's convenient. What can you tell me about Tony Redding's firm?"

"I've already told you too much."

She waved off his concern. "I can always do an internet search, but it'll be a lot easier and faster if you just tell me. It's not a secret, is it?"

"You haven't changed a bit," he said.

"Oh, I have. Believe me, I have. But we're talking about Tony Redding."

"He's the cofounder and CEO of Redding Technologies. They develop apps for the military. Everything from navigation to beacons to handbooks and probably a whole lot more that they don't advertise. It's a competitive field, and from what I gather, they devour start-ups for breakfast."

"He's made enemies, then."

"I think that's safe to say."

Ava turned once more to stare out the window as she pondered his revelations. He was irritated with himself for succumbing so easily to her interrogation, but he'd told her nothing she couldn't have found out on her own. The trick now was to keep her at arm's length from the case. That wouldn't be easy. She'd always been single-minded to a fault. With her intellect and ambition, she'd been a force of nature even in college. He'd meant it earlier when he said she hadn't changed. If anything, she was even more driven.

He studied her profile now as memories assailed him. He'd known her for years, but their time as a couple had been brief and mostly clandestine. Her choice. She'd thought it best to keep their feelings secret until Lily had had time to process the breakup and move on. Looking back now, Dylan realized that had been a mistake. They'd done nothing wrong, but keeping their relationship from the others made it seem as if they had. They'd both learned the hard way that trust built on a foundation of secrets and lies could too easily crumble away.

Still, he'd never been able to forget her even in the fog of war. He'd spent many a sleepless night looking up at the stars in a desert sky and longing for the familiarity of her touch, her smile. The feel of her body against his. For a while, it was all that had kept him going. Eventually he'd put all those memories aside, buried them in the deepest recesses of his mind while he'd concentrated on the task at hand. On surviving. When he finally came home, he'd had too many other things to think about. Too many monsters to vanquish.

But now here she was, mere inches from his arms.

He skimmed her hungrily, admiring the way her sweater and slacks molded to her soft curves. She wore heels and the subtlest of perfumes, something woodsy and exotic, and he thought, *damn*. How could he have forgotten Ava North even for a moment?

"Did you hear what I said?" she demanded.

"What?"

"You're a million miles away," she accused.

"Nope. Right here with you." He tried to shake off his bewitchment. "You said something's not right."

"Okay, so you were listening." She rested her hand on a chair back. "I don't know how to explain it, but earlier I had the strangest feeling while we were in that room with Blair. She was obviously distressed and she said all the appropriate things, but something was off. Something wasn't right. Am I crazy?"

"You're not crazy."

Her eyes widened as she stared at him. "You felt it, too?"

"You're not crazy."

"I'll take that as a yes. I've been standing here thinking back to our college days."

A dangerous journey, Dylan knew only too well. "In general or something specific?"

"Both. Tony Redding was never really part of our group, but he was around a lot because of Blair. He seemed like a good guy on the surface, but for some reason, I could never warm up to him. I always had a feeling there was a lot more going on inside that he didn't want anyone to see."

Dylan gave her an ironic smile. "You used to say the same thing about me."

She trailed a finger across the back of the chair. "That was different."

"How?"

"It just was. Tony's ambiguity seemed nefarious. Like he had something to hide. He was charming and solicitous until he reeled Blair in, and then he changed. She did, too. Don't you remember what she was like before he came along? So happy and outgoing. Once Tony entered the picture, she faded somehow. It was like she disappeared into his shadow."

"Are you sure you aren't relying too much on your recall? College was a long time ago," Dylan said. "A lot's happened since then."

"Maybe I am. Maybe my uneasiness comes from being back in this place. Seeing Blair again. Seeing you again." She broke off, biting her lip as if she'd let something slip, revealing her own uncertainty. Almost against her will, her voice softened and she grew reminiscent. "Do you remember slipping down to the springs the last time we were here? It was a hot night, but the water was cool and so crystal clear, you could see moonlight glinting off the silt and limestone bottom. We floated on our backs for the longest time, just gazing up at the stars."

"I remember everything." The taste of her, the scent of her, their forbidden promises.

She dropped her gaze to the floor as if she were thinking the same thing. "Anyway, Blair always had to work so hard for Tony's attention. He seemed to put everything and everyone before her, as if she were an afterthought. I remember once she tried to plan a trip to South Padre for spring break. She made all the arrangements, and then Tony told her at the last minute that he wanted to go skiing with his buddies. She never let on how upset she was. She just smiled and shrugged off her disappointment. Then the night before he was scheduled to leave, she was mugged on her way home from the library. The assailant knocked her to the ground, put a knife to her throat and threatened to kill her if she screamed. He grabbed her purse and ran off. By the time any of us heard about the incident, Tony had canceled his trip to be with her. The two of them ended up going to Cancun alone."

"I remember when she was mugged," Dylan said. "But I'm not sure where you're going with this."

"She was very upset, and she seemed skittish for a long time after the attack. But here's the thing. I was with her at the library that night and I remember distinctly her red leather handbag. It was very expensive and she'd coveted it for a long time before her mother finally broke down and bought it for her. A few months after the incident, Blair offered to loan me a dress for a formal event. I saw that same handbag in her closet."

"Maybe her mother bought a replacement."

"That's possible."

"Or maybe the police found her bag and returned it."

"Also possible."

"But you don't think so. Did you ask her about it?"

"No." Ava made a helpless gesture with her hand. "Maybe I didn't really want to know. But I had the same feeling that day in her apartment that I had earlier in her suite. Something was off. Maybe I was wrong then and maybe I'm wrong now. But, Dylan…"

"Yes?"

"Be careful, okay? My instincts are pretty good these days."

"You think I'm being played?"

"Just…be careful."

"I will."

She nodded, absently running a hand up and down her arm as if suddenly chilled. "I should get back downstairs. The others are probably waiting." But she made no move to the door.

"Something else on your mind?"

She looked as if she wanted to flee, but instead she held her ground. Her head came up, and Dylan watched in fascination as her expression shifted.

"Why did you lie to me earlier when we spoke on the terrace? Working for a private security firm is hardly being at loose ends." Her tone was more curious than reproachful.

"It wasn't my place to tell you the real reason I'm here, but I didn't lie. There are times when I do still feel at loose ends."

"You don't like your job?"

"It has nothing to do with the job." He hesitated, uncertain how much he wanted to reveal about his current frame of mind. "It's hard to explain, but when you come back from combat deployment, there's a feeling of disassociation. Maybe *displacement* is a better word. Like you don't really belong here anymore. Like you don't belong anywhere. It doesn't go away overnight."

"I'm sorry."

"Don't be. You asked and I'm trying to explain, but I'm not complaining. I'm lucky I made it back at all. But it takes a while to feel normal again. No one tells you how to get your old life back."

No one tells you that even little things like sleeping in a real bed and eating meals at regular hours require an adjustment. You become so accustomed to operating on hyperalert that boredom can easily set in even in the middle of a task. You find yourself restless and anxious at the most inopportune times. And then when you think you've finally reintegrated, the nightmares return and you wake up thinking about the friends you lost and the ones who are still over there, the ones who won't ever come home. You hear about a suicide and then another and before you know it, you're back in a very dark place.

"Dylan?"

He pulled himself away from the edge. "Yeah?"

Her voice softened. "Why do I get the feeling you're still not telling me the whole story?"

"I wouldn't want to bore you."

"As if you ever could."

He felt sucker punched by her smile. "Give it time."

Her expression sobered. "I'm glad you're home. I'm glad you're safe."

"Thanks."

She looked around as if searching for a graceful exit. "I really should get going."

He caught her arm as she started for the door. The action surprised him as much as it seemed to surprise her. She lifted her head, searching his face, but she didn't try to pull away.

"Really. Thank you."

Her eyes deepened as she gazed up at him. "For what?"

"For caring, I guess."

"This may come as a surprise, but I never really stopped."

AVA FLED TO HER ROOM, flinging herself on the bed for a moment before rising to splash cold water on her face. She ruined her makeup and had to reapply, but it gave her something to focus on besides Dylan Burkhart. Besides her pounding heart.

What had she been thinking, going to his room alone, putting herself through a second confrontation when it would be so much easier for her peace of mind if she simply avoided him? Whispering Springs was a big place. She could get through the next few days without another one-on-one. The last thing she needed was to succumb to old memories, and even worse, to become ensnared in another of Blair's intrigues. Ava had her own problems. Let Dylan handle the Reddings. This trip was supposed to be all about rest and relaxation. A reset, so to speak, so that she could go back to Houston and get on with her work.

She drew a long breath as she scrutinized her reflection. She was still a young woman, vital and attractive, but suddenly she saw nothing but flaws—the careless ponytail, the jaded set of her mouth, the faint circles beneath her eyes from too many late nights.

What did Dylan see when he looked at her?

She supposed it was only natural to wonder about one's impact on an ex. Ten years was a long time, and Ava hadn't been a particularly fastidious guardian of her mental and physical well-being. She worked out religiously but she also ate junk food and drank too much coffee. She spent too many hours at the office and took work home on weekends. She never got to bed before midnight and often rose before dawn. That kind of abuse was bound to show up sooner or later in her face and on her hips.

But Dylan. Even after everything he'd been through, he still looked amazing.

She braced her hands on either side of the sink, still peering into the mirror, but she no longer saw her reflection. Instead she conjured an image of Dylan on the day she'd sent him away. He'd been hurt and angry by her rejection, refusing to take on the burden of guilt that had shattered her after Lily's death. But Ava had remained adamant. How could they go on together after hurting someone they both loved so deeply?

Now she could look back on the tragedy more objectively. Neither she nor Dylan had been responsible for what happened to Lily. They hadn't betrayed her. They hadn't set out to hurt her. They'd simply fallen in love. But Ava had used her guilt as an excuse to break things off. In part because she'd cared too much about what the others would think of her, but mostly because the notion of a long-term commitment had terrified her. Still did. Funny how clearly she could see that now. Fear of heights wasn't her only phobia.

Uncapping her lipstick, she started to reapply, then paused, tube in hand, as she thought about the message that had been left on Blair's mirror. *Tell the truth.* And she thought once more of that broken doll so carefully arranged on Blair's bed. Maybe Dylan was right and the incidents were nothing more than hardball intimidation from a business rival, but try as she might, she couldn't dismiss a lingering disquiet that all was not as it seemed.

She put away her makeup, rinsed her hands and returned to the bedroom, stepping back into her heels as she moved toward the balcony doors. She went outside for a breath of fresh air to steady her nerves before facing the others. Celeste would be easy. She had always been a free spirit, the perfect counterpoint to Ava's ambition. Blair was the organizer and Lily had been the dreamer. Jane was the one Ava dreaded facing the most. Quiet and intense, she had remained on the fringes of the group, never quite in, never quite out, an inscrutable presence that had always made Ava just a little uncomfortable.

And then there was Tony, the ruthless businessman, and Dylan, the enigmatic protector.

The evening loomed before her as she scanned the deepening horizon. The moon was up, along with a few scattered stars. A light breeze blew across the balcony, carrying the scent of the evergreens. If she turned her head just right, she could hear the whispers drifting up from the springs. The sound was at once eerie and seductive, like a siren's call from the other side. Ava drew in another fortifying breath before turning to go back inside.

A movement at the corner of her eye stopped her and she spun back to the railing, searching the darkness that had gathered at the edge of the woods. She thought at first it must be nothing more than a branch moving around in the breeze or a wild animal that had become used to human encroachment.

But the longer she stared, the more convinced she became that someone lurked just beyond the spill of light, hidden by the deepest part of the shadows. She could just make out a silhouette.

Someone was out there watching her. Watching them all, perhaps.

Fear prickled her spine as she backed toward the door, her gaze fixed on the shadow. She had the urge to call out to the lurker, to demand to know the person's identity and their business at the ranch. Instead, she remained silent and frozen until the howl of a coyote sent her fleeing to the safety of her room.

She closed and locked the door and then pulled the drapes, shutting out the night and those prying eyes.

Chapter Five

Ava was surprised to find the great room still deserted when she returned downstairs, though the long table in the dining room had been set with gleaming china and crystal and she could smell tantalizing scents from the kitchen.

The French doors stood open to the terrace, where candles now flickered in the evening breeze. Citronella torches had been lit all along the walkways, casting ghostly shadows across the grounds and into the edge of the woods. Ava wondered if she'd seen one of those dancing shadows earlier and if she'd let her imagination get the better of her.

Even so, she stepped outside with more than a little trepidation, advancing to the very edge of the patio but no farther. Removing the small flashlight she'd put in her bag earlier, she aimed the beam across the lawn and all along the tree line. Satisfied that nothing seemed amiss, she moved out from under the lattice covering so that she could scan the second-floor balconies.

Blair's suite was directly above her and still brightly lit, the drapes still open to the night. A softer light glowed from the room at the end, but the middle room remained dark. Dylan's room was on the opposite side of the house. Was he still up there? Ava wondered. Or was he out scouring the grounds looking for evidence of an intruder?

Slowly she pivoted back to the woods, refocusing the beam on the trees. All remained quiet and calm, but she had the strangest feeling that she was far from alone.

"Ava?"

She'd been so intent on her mission that she hadn't heard anyone approach. Now she whirled in surprise at the sound of her name, and the flashlight beam swept across the newcomer's face before Ava quickly doused the light.

"Jane?" Ava moved back to the patio. "I almost didn't recognize you. It's been a long time, and you look so different with short hair."

"Do I?" The young woman fingered the fringe at her nape.

"It's quite a change for someone who was once known on campus as the girl with the hair."

"I could sit on it back then."

"I remember. But the short style suits you. I like it."

During the exchange, Jane had remained in the doorway, as if reluctant to commit to a full-fledged reunion. Then, with an almost imperceptible shrug, she walked across the terrace to lean against the railing, her gaze roaming the darkness. Ava came up beside her, wrapping her hand around a cedar post as she gave the woman a sidelong scrutiny. Candlelight and the subtle glow of overhead lanterns cast Jane in a soft spotlight, and Ava realized that the haircut wasn't the only change. Jane had traded in her jeans and the thrift store tops she'd favored in college for an exquisitely cut shift dress. Ava also recognized the designer sandals that fastened around Jane's slender ankles and the buttery gleam of gold bracelets that jangled at her wrists.

Ava wasn't surprised by Jane's apparent prosperity. She had always been an over-achiever. What took Ava aback was the sly smile that curled at the corners of Jane's lips as she gazed out into the darkness. An old saying came to mind: *The cat that swallowed the canary.*

Unease bristled again as Ava turned back to the grounds.

"What were you looking for just now?" Jane asked.

"I'm sorry?"

She nodded to the flashlight that Ava still gripped. "It appeared you were searching for something when I first saw you. You were running the flashlight beam all along the trees."

"Oh, that." She returned the flashlight to her bag. "I thought I saw something earlier at the edge of the woods. Possibly a deer." Or an intruder. A watcher. It was all Ava could do to suppress another shiver.

"More likely a coyote," Jane said. "They've been going crazy ever since I got here, and it seems they get closer every night. It's like they can smell the tension."

"What tension?"

The canary-eating grin flashed again. "You'll find out soon enough."

Jane moved out from underneath the lattice, turning first to the woods and then lifting her head toward the escarpment. With torchlight shimmering across her narrow, pointy features, she looked elfin and feral, and Ava couldn't help but reflect again on the shattered doll that had been left on Blair's bed. What if the effigy had nothing at all to do with business and everything to do with a grudge that someone in their group had held all these years?

"So there's tension in the ranks," Ava said, keeping her voice light. "Don't tell me Celeste and Blair are at each other's throats already."

"I'd forgotten about their petty squabbles," Jane said. "They act so chummy one moment, and then the next, you'd think they're the bitterest of enemies. Alone, I find Blair mildly annoying, but when she's with Celeste, they're both insufferable."

Ava laughed. "They've always been very dramatic and impossibly competitive. We all were, as I recall. But they had their moments."

"Why do you feel the need to defend

them?" Jane asked. "You're not at all like them. You have substance. I've always wondered how you could be friends with such shallow, narcissistic women."

Ava turned in surprise. "They were your friends, too."

"Not really."

"Why would you say that? We were all close in college."

"If you're trying to spare my feelings, you needn't bother," Jane said airily. "I know I was the odd man out and I'm totally fine with that. Looking back, I can't think of a single thing I had in common with any of you."

"Then why are you here?" Ava didn't bother to soften her bluntness.

Jane shrugged. "Curiosity. Boredom. Unfinished business."

Ava tried to keep her tone even as she watched Jane closely. "What kind of unfinished business?"

"You know."

"No, I don't know. Why don't you just say what you mean?"

Jane took a step toward her, and Ava fought the urge to retreat. Something in her tone, in her whole demeanor set off too many alarm bells, but the voice of reason intervened. Jane was an old friend. She'd always been opaque and enigmatic, but it was crazy to think she could actually be dangerous. Wasn't it?

As if sensing Ava's disquiet, Jane stopped short and turned back to the cliffs, tucking both hands into her dress pockets. She drew in a long breath and slowly exhaled as if releasing pent-up tension. "As a group, we never really dealt with Lily's suicide. Oh, we cried and grieved, but then we just swept our collective guilt under a rug and got on with our lives as if nothing had happened. As if she never really mattered."

"That's not true. Her death hit us all hard."

"Some harder than others, perhaps."

Her insinuation annoyed Ava. "You think now is the time to revisit what happened to Lily? After all these years?"

"Don't you still think about her?" Was that the slightest edge of accusation in Jane's voice?

"Of course I think about her. I just don't dwell. I don't see how dredging up the past will do anyone any good."

"Isn't that the point of a reunion?"

Ava shrugged. "I thought the point was to catch up and reconnect. Maybe have a little fun."

Jane laughed, a low, humorless sound. "You really think this is going to be a fun get-together?"

"I'm trying to remain optimistic."

Jane fell silent for a moment, her gaze still on Ava. "Do you remember that game we used to play?"

"The Game of Secrets," Ava said. "Of course I remember. It was our version of Truth or Dare. Take a drink, reveal a secret."

"Take lots of drinks, reveal your deepest, darkest secret—or someone else's. We played the night before Lily died. We never played again."

"It seemed too frivolous. Besides, we all went our separate ways after graduation."

"I've always wondered if something exposed during that last game triggered Lily. Things got a little out of hand. People said things they shouldn't have."

"We'll never know." Ava watched the play of shadows across Jane's face. "I don't think any one thing triggered Lily. She was obviously wrestling with something dark that none of us knew about."

"Another rug, more sweeping," Jane said.

"I suppose that's one way of looking at it."

Jane gave her a long appraisal. "Can I ask you something? I was told you weren't coming. What changed your mind?"

"I needed a break from work and the invitation was timely. And I only had to travel from Houston," Ava couldn't resist adding. "You've come a long way to spend time with people you don't like."

"Didn't anyone tell you? I'm back in Austin. I have been for a few years now. The company I worked for went under, so there was nothing keeping me in California."

"I had no idea. I guess you must see Blair now and then."

"Once or twice. We belong to the same rock climbing community, but we don't socialize."

"A rock climbing community. My goodness. That sounds intimidating."

Jane's smile turned sly once more. "I take it you don't intend to climb while we're here?"

Ava leaned a shoulder against the post and folded her arms. "Nope, still not a fan of heights. I'd like to hike the canyon, though. I always enjoyed that."

"Hiking can be just as dangerous as climbing. Did you know that a girl vanished from one of the trails when this place first opened? Her name was Sara."

"Funny you should mention her," Ava said. "The driver and I were just talking about that disappearance on the way here from the airport."

"You mean Noah Pickett? He's more than a driver. He helps run this place. He does a bit of everything, including tour guide."

Ava nodded. "Yes, I got that impression. Anyway, as I remember the story, the police thought the woman met with foul play."

"Oh, I don't think she was murdered." Jane's slyness lingered as she walked back to the patio. "I think she was swallowed up by something far more powerful."

A chill prickled along Ava's spine. "What do you mean?"

Jane lifted her face to the night. "Can't you feel it? There's something unnatural about this place. Maybe it's the way the water whispers over the rocks or the lights that flicker at the top of Bishop's Rock." Moonlight glinted in her eyes. "They say you can still hear Sara's screams echoing up from the canyon when the wind blows just right."

Ava tried not to react to the strange current in Jane's voice, to the almost primal glow in her eyes. If she was deliberately trying to spook her, she was doing a very good job. "I don't think there was anything supernatural about the disappearance. Human monsters are the ones to be feared."

"And yet you were out here in the dark, searching for something with your flashlight," Jane said. "And I saw Dylan Burkhart up on the cliffs earlier with his binoculars. If I were the suspicious type, I might think the two of you know something the rest of us don't."

"What could that possibly be?"

"You tell me."

Ava glanced away, scouring the shadows as a comment Dylan had once made came back to her: *"Have you ever noticed how possessive Jane is of Lily?"*

"They're friends, Dylan. I don't see anything unusual about her behavior."

"Come on, she's like a shadow. She even

tries to dress like Lily. It's not flattery. It's possessive and creepy."

"That's not a very nice thing to say about one of our friends."

"I don't think Jane is a very nice person."

Ava hadn't thought about that conversation in years. So many memories had been forgotten in the wake of Lily's suicide and Dylan's defection. Now another conversation came back to her. She and Jane were in the car heading for the airport a few days after graduation. They had both been silent and morose for most of the journey, each lost in gloomy thoughts. But as they neared the airport, Jane had turned to her suddenly.

"Do you think she felt any pain?"

"I don't know, Jane. I try not to think about it. I hope it was over instantly."

"But there would have been a moment. An excruciating flash—"

"It's best not to dwell."

"I can't help it. I close my eyes and I see her up on that roof, alone and desperate. No one to talk to. Nowhere to turn. She reached out for help, but we let her down. All of us. And now we have to live with that, don't we?

Those last texts she sent haunt me, Ava. If even one of us had bothered to find her—"

"Don't, Jane."

"I wonder what went through her mind when no one came. Who she thought about before she jumped."

"I'm worried about you, Janie. You haven't been yourself since the funeral. I understand why you feel the need to get away, but don't get on that plane. It's too soon. You shouldn't be alone right now. None of us should."

"But we are alone, Ava. Don't you get that? You, me, the others. Peel away the masks and we're nothing more than strangers. We hide behind our secrets and lies because none of us are who we say we are."

"So this is where everyone is hiding out."

Ava turned in relief at the sound of Celeste Matthews's throaty voice. An awkward silence had settled over the patio in the wake of all those old memories and Jane's enigmatic musings.

Celeste glanced from one to the other. "I'm not interrupting anything, am I?"

"Of course not," Ava said a shade too enthusiastically. "Come join us."

"If you insist." Celeste's perfume wafted

on the breeze as she stepped onto the patio. She was dressed in sleek white pants and a chartreuse top that bared her pale shoulders. She leaned her forearms against the railing as she glanced out over the grounds. "I'd forgotten how beautiful the Hill Country is at night. All those woodsy smells and a million stars overhead. There's something rejuvenating about the air here. Almost like a spiritual awakening."

"It is a lovely evening," Ava agreed, although she didn't share either woman's observation about spiritual awakenings and uncanny feelings. She did sense something out of place, though. Something that wasn't quite right. She turned once again to scan the tree line.

"Better enjoy it while we can," Celeste said. "According to the weather channel, there's a storm front heading our way."

"A bad one?" Ava asked.

She shrugged. "Who knows? Mother Nature is nothing if not unpredictable. I'm just glad you came when you did. Enough rain and the roads around here become impassable. The reunion wouldn't have been the same without you."

"I doubt that's true, but it's nice of you to say so."

"No, I mean it. And it's really good to have some new blood around this place, right, Janie?"

"No one calls me that anymore," Jane said. She had grown sullen ever since Celeste's arrival, and now Ava detected an unpleasant undercurrent in the woman's tone. She thought again of Dylan's observation that Jane had had an unhealthy attachment to Lily. *Possessive and creepy*.

"As beautiful as this place is, the isolation can get to you," Celeste said. "Maybe I'm just used to sleeping through all the French Quarter noise, but the silence here can be a little unsettling. And the days are interminable."

"Interminable? And here I thought you'd be in your element," Ava said. "You used to love to hike and climb. Not to mention the spa."

"Yes, the spa is wonderful. As for the rest, my outdoor skills are rusty these days. I've been in the city too long. I did some climbing in the lower canyon yesterday, and today my muscles hate me for it."

"You don't plan to climb Bishop's Rock?"

Jane asked. "That's a shame. I guess I'll have to race Blair to the top, then."

Celeste gave her a hard scrutiny. "Since when did you become such an ardent climber? As I recall, you used to hide behind Ava's acrophobia."

"I've been climbing for years," Jane said. "Boulder Canyon, the Pinnacle. Bishop's Rock shouldn't be much of a challenge."

Celeste smiled. "Careful, Janie. We all know what happens to climbers who get too cocky."

Jane bristled but before she could reply, Ava cut her off. "Enough about climbing. Who's ready for a drink?"

"Now you're talking." Celeste curled her arm through Ava's. "You coming, Janie?"

She said coolly, "No, but you two go on. I'll just hang back and wait for the fireworks."

They were barely out of earshot before Celeste muttered, "That smug little witch. Has she always had that attitude and I just forgot?"

"She's seems a little more caustic than I remembered. As for attitude, you've always been able to give as good as you got."

Celeste scowled over her shoulder. "True,

but I still say someone needs to take her down a peg or two."

"Well, you've got the rest of the week to work on that," Ava said, with her own acerbic edge. "What exactly did she mean by fireworks?"

"Oh, that. There was an incident the first night I got here. Blair and I had too much to drink and things got a little tense."

"More tense than what I just witnessed on the patio?"

Celeste smiled. "Jane's an ankle biter. Blair goes for the jugular."

"And here I was hoping for a restful retreat."

"Whatever gave you such a foolish notion? Should we start with tequila?"

"Tempting," Ava said. "But I think wine, at least until after dinner."

"I'll see what I can rustle up." Celeste walked over to the dining room doorway and motioned to one of the staff. A young man returned almost instantly with two glasses of Texas merlot. She handed one of the stems to Ava. "What should we drink to? The good old days?"

"How about surviving the week without any major casualties?"

They clinked glasses and sipped.

"You know, of course, I'll have to climb Bishop's Rock now," Celeste said.

"Why? You said your outdoor skills are rusty."

"I don't have a choice. Jane threw down the gauntlet and I can't have her thinking she could best me." Her eyes sparkled with anticipation.

"You're being ridiculous," Ava said.

"This whole reunion is ridiculous. Why are we even here, Ava? How did we let Blair talk us into this?"

"Because Blair always gets her way."

"True enough, unfortunately." Celeste's expression hardened as she glanced over Ava's shoulder. "And why is *he* always staring at me?"

"Who?" Ava turned, almost expecting to find that Dylan had returned from another scouting excursion. Instead, Noah, the driver, stood in the archway, his gaze fixed on Celeste. "Looks like someone has a little crush," she teased.

Celeste wrinkled her nose. "A little too rough around the edges for my taste."

"He seems nice."

"I'm sure he's perfectly lovely," Celeste said. "But I prefer more polish." Her gaze turned pensive. "Does he seem familiar to you, Ava? I swear I've seen him before, but I can't place where. It's been driving me crazy ever since I got here."

"Maybe that's why he's been staring at you. He recognizes you, too. Did you ask him where your paths might have crossed?"

"He said he has one of those faces, but I don't think that's it." She spared him another glance and shrugged. "Oh, well. I'll figure it out."

"Wish I could help, but I never laid eyes on him until he picked me up at the airport." Even before the words were out of Ava's mouth, déjà vu shivered up her spine. Her gaze met Noah's across the room and for a moment, she sensed a subtle hostility that hadn't been apparent on the drive from the airport. Then he nodded and turned to disappear through another doorway. "Maybe you're right," she murmured. "Maybe we have seen him somewhere before."

"See? I told you. I never forget a face. Anyway, I did find out something interesting about him. Did you know his family used to own this ranch?"

"Really? He never said anything to me about it on the drive here."

"Nor to me. I heard it from someone else. Apparently, Whispering Springs had been in his family for generations. The Picketts fell on hard times and had to sell to a developer. The bank eventually foreclosed on the new owner and that's when Tony Redding and his group swooped in."

"Tony Redding? He owns this place? I thought Blair just rented it for the week. When did all this happen?"

"Years ago. I'm sure Blair must have mentioned it."

"If she did, it slipped my mind."

"Or you weren't really listening in the first place," Celeste accused. "I always had a feeling you were tuning us out."

"That's not true."

Celeste merely smiled at the denial. "Say what you will about Tony, but the man knows how to spot a diamond in the rough."

"Maybe the ranch is where we've seen

Noah," Ava suggested. "If his family still owned Whispering Springs when we first started coming out here, he was probably around at some point."

"Yes, I thought of that," Celeste said. "And it does seem a logical explanation, but I don't think that's it, either. Like I said, it'll come to me sooner or later."

"I wonder what it's like for him to work here now," Ava mused.

"Maybe it's a relief not to have to worry about the finances. Something to be said for leaving the job behind when you go home at the end of the day."

"I wouldn't know," Ava muttered. "If Tony bought this place a few years ago, then he must have been the owner when that girl disappeared."

Celeste's gaze sharpened. "What girl?"

"Her name was Sara. She worked here when the place first opened. According to Noah, she went out to walk the trails after her shift one day and was never seen or heard from again. He implied the police tried to build a case against her boyfriend so as to avoid any adverse publicity for the newly opened retreat."

"That wouldn't surprise me. Tony isn't above greasing a few palms."

Ava lifted a brow. "You sound as if you still know him pretty well."

"I suppose I know him as well as I know you or Jane or Blair. Which is to say, not well at all these days."

"Have you kept in touch with Blair since the three of us stopped meeting?"

"We've only just recently reconnected. I'd forgotten how high maintenance she tends to be. More so now than ever."

Ava said carefully, "Do you know why?"

Celeste glanced around the room and then leaned in. "You didn't hear any of this from me."

"Of course not."

"Blair has been trying to get pregnant. All the women in her circle are having babies, and you know how competitive she is. She views her infertility as a personal failure."

"That's crazy."

"That's Blair." Celeste smoothed a hand across her middle. "She probably thinks having a child will keep Tony from straying, but between you and me, that ship sailed a long time ago. I've never thought they were suited to one another anyway. Blair's far too needy."

"She must be doing something right. They've been together for a long time."

"Well, she is the one with all the money."

Ava lifted a brow. "Meaning Tony is still with her because of her inheritance? Come on. We're not that cynical, are we?"

Irritation flashed in Celeste's eyes. "She's also a very good manipulator, but sooner or later, people catch on."

"By people, you mean Tony?"

She gave Ava a strange look. "Enough about Blair. Tell me about you."

More questions churned, but Ava forced them back with a smile. "Not much to tell. I'm a single workaholic."

"You're not seeing anyone right now? Surely there must be someone out there who floats your boat."

"Maybe, but I'm not looking."

"Well, who knows? You could get lucky while you're here, although the prospects are thin at best. There's always Dylan Burkhart. I understand he's free."

Ava tried to act casual, but her pulse quickened at the mere mention of his name.

"Maybe you should just worry about your own love life."

"Oh, that's covered, don't worry." Celeste sipped her wine thoughtfully. "Don't get mad, but I always thought you and Dylan had a little something going on. I sensed a vibe after he and Lily broke up. Was I wrong?"

Ava lifted her glass and pretended to sip as she contemplated her response. Why not just tell the truth—that she had been madly in love with Dylan Burkhart even before he'd broken things off with Lily? Why was she still keeping secrets after all these years? Did she really care that much about Celeste's opinion of her? Or was she too frightened to admit to herself that she might still carry a torch?

"That was a long time ago," she said. "There might have been a spark, but it hardly matters now. We're strangers. And anyway, after what happened to Lily…"

"Oh, I know. That's a cross we all still bear." Celeste stared into her glass with a heavy sigh. "Lily's secrets died with her that night, but the rest of us have had to live with ours."

Ava glanced up. "What secrets?"

A shadow darkened Celeste's features before she turned away. "None of us ever revealed all our secrets, no matter what we pretended. I didn't, you didn't." She paused. "Lily wasn't the innocent she pretended to be during those games we used to play. Let's just leave it at that. It's bad luck to speak ill of the dead."

A FEW HOURS LATER, Dylan let himself into his room, relieved the social portion of the evening had finally come to an end. He'd been seated across the table from Ava at dinner, and he'd had to use all his willpower to stay focused on the idle chitchat around him.

After they finished eating, Blair had ushered everyone into the great room for coffee and cordials. But her mind had seemed elsewhere and she'd spent the remainder of the evening checking her phone and staring out the front windows. Tony hadn't arrived at his scheduled time, and Blair had grown progressively agitated as the evening wore on, even though he'd called to say he would be delayed.

Ava was the first to excuse herself, pleading fatigue and a headache. Jane had gone up next, leaving Dylan to referee Blair and Celeste. Finally, Blair had given up on Tony's arrival and retired to her suite, and Celeste had gone out for a quick stroll. Dylan had watched her from the patio. She'd walked down the drive just out of earshot and lingered in the shadows to make a phone call. Dylan was too far away to catch any of the conversation, but something about her furtive movements had put him on alert. He waited until she'd gone up to her room and then made his nightly rounds.

All was quiet inside the house. Most of the staff had gone home for the night. Upon check-in, guests were issued keys to the outside entrances along with their room keys. They could come and go as they pleased, but if anyone made the mistake of locking themselves out after ten, they would be at the mercy of their fellow visitors.

Dylan eased down the hallway, stopping at the unoccupied room to press his ear against the door. No sound came to him and the door remained locked. He continued down the corridor. He could hear music coming from Jane's room and the TV from Celeste's. All was silent in Ava's quarters, but still Dylan lingered. He even lifted his hand to knock, then quickly dropped it to his side, annoyed with himself for his lapse as he continued down the hallway to his room.

Shedding his jacket, he kicked off his shoes and lay down on top of the covers. He was too wired to sleep, or so he thought, but the next thing he knew, a sound awakened him and he bolted upright. He rose from bed and moved silently to the door, cracking it open to peer both ways down the corridor. Satisfied that all was well, he went out onto the balcony. It was a dark night. The moon was up but low-lying clouds muted the glow. The torches along the driveway had been extinguished and the security lights around the building's perimeter barely breached the shadows along the tree line.

Something was wrong. Dylan could feel it in the warning tingle at the base of his spine, in the bristle of hair at his nape. He went back inside to slip on his shoes and retrieve his weapon from the nightstand. Then he moved back to the balcony, pressing against the wall as he scanned the grounds, peering into the trees and all along the escarpment. Seconds passed before he finally spotted something out of the ordinary. A car was parked just inside the arched entrance facing the ranch. The driver had pulled to the side of the road where the vehicle would be concealed by shadows.

Dylan could just make out a silhouette moving quickly away from the house. As the clouds parted, moonlight shimmered down through the leaves, painting the intruder with a silvery haze as she glanced back at the ranch. It was Celeste.

She was dressed in dark clothing that made her nearly invisible against the night. As if sensing Dylan's scrutiny, her head came up as she scanned the second-story balconies. For a moment, he could have sworn their gazes collided. He remained motionless until she turned back to the drive.

Of all the people assembled at Whispering Springs, Dylan knew the least about Celeste. They had never been close in college, and as he had with the rest of the group, he'd lost track of her after graduation. But a background check revealed that up until a year ago, she'd been a partner in an upscale clothing boutique in New Orleans. She'd left abruptly, and despite the fact that she had no visible means of support, she rented an expensive apartment in the French Quarter and drove a late model Mercedes convertible. Her extravagant lifestyle could be chalked up to the sale of the boutique or even an inheritance, but her lack of a digital footprint had raised a flag for Dylan. She was a social media ghost.

Which made him wonder what she might be hiding as he watched her slip along the driveway. She was still several yards from the car when the headlights flashed on and off. Clearly a signal, but the brilliance seemed to catch her off guard and she froze like a deer.

Dylan heard the engine start up and then the low rumble of a powerful motor as the car eased toward Celeste. She moved to the curb and waited for the vehicle to pull alongside her. She and the driver conversed for a moment and then, as she stepped away from the car, an arm shot through the open window to grab her. She flung off the hand and stumbled back. The car door opened and in the brief flare from the dome light, Dylan recognized Tony Redding.

He lunged out of the car so quickly Celeste had no time to evade him. He gripped her arm and spun her to face him. Her hand came up to slap him and a frenzied scuffle ensued.

Dylan had seen enough. He climbed over the balcony railing and dropped silently to the ground. Slipping along the row of cedars, he kept to the shadows so as not to be seen. But by the time he was close enough to hear their muted voices, the confrontation was over. Tony got back in the car, slammed the door and revved the engine with little regard for discretion. The car tore up the drive and peeled around to the back of the house, where Dylan had parked earlier. The ignition was turned off and the door slammed again.

Celeste had remained at the curb, head cocked, her expression enigmatic as she listened to his departure. Then, drawing a long breath, she followed Tony back to the ranch.

Chapter Six

The next morning, most of the group, including Dylan, set out bright and early for Bishop's Rock. Ava declined the invitation to join them. Climbing up four hundred feet of granite was nowhere to be found on her bucket list. Nor did she care to wait at the base and watch their ascent. The memory of Dylan's fall was still too vivid and besides, now that she'd been forced into this quasi-vacation, the idea of having a morning all to herself didn't sound so bad.

Normally she would have holed up in her room with her laptop and a gallon of coffee, taking in the magnificent Hill Country scenery through a window. But she had her orders, and maybe time away from her work really would do her some good. The sun felt wonderful on her face and the scent from the evergreens was intoxicating as she headed out. She resisted a brief urge to call the office and instead put her phone on mute and zipped it in the pocket of her hoodie.

A well-worn path gently sloped to the bottom of the canyon, and Ava took her time descending, admiring the splashes of blooming cacti that grew in craggy crevices. Here and there, she could spot carved-out openings in the rock that led back into narrow caves, none of which she had any intention of exploring.

The day soon grew warm and balmy and she shed her hoodie, tying the sleeves around her waist as she picked her way along the rugged trail. She'd never been much of an outdoor person, preferring even in college to camp out in the library or snuggle in bed with a good book. But she had always enjoyed searching for arrowheads and fossils, those bits of history hidden in the gravel at the bottom of dry riverbeds.

With the sun beating down on her bare shoulders, an unexpected harmony settled over her. She walked farther than she intended, stopping now and then to sift through pebbles and stones and stowing found treasure in her backpack.

She might have kept going, allowing the fresh air to wash away her work worries and any lingering thoughts of Dylan, but the first sprinkles of rain stopped her in her tracks. She lifted her head to warily scan the sky.

Celeste had made it sound as though the storm system was still days away, but already clouds gathered overhead and a strong wind blew down through the canyon. Ava listened for a moment, wondering if she might hear poor Sara's phantom screams. But at the moment, Noah Pickett's urban legend was the least of her concerns.

Ava was Texas born and raised and no stranger to abrupt weather changes. The clouds didn't overly worry her, but she knew better than to get trapped at the bottom of a canyon in a rainstorm. Shrugging into her sweatshirt, she pulled up the hood before reluctantly heading back, not anxious for the company of the others. She had the fanciful notion that if she just kept going, she might walk herself right out of that reunion. She had no wish to be caught up in all those petty little intrigues and grievances. Let them sort out their own problems.

Still, she couldn't help but reflect on the doll that had been left on Blair's bed and Tony's refusal to call the police. His willfulness made no sense to Ava, particularly after a home break-in. An investigation should have been launched after the first threatening phone call, but Blair had had to go behind her husband's back to hire protection.

Ava told herself she was being too cynical. A reunion of old friends was bound to stir bad memories and ill feelings. But she couldn't shake the notion that beneath the tranquility of Whispering Springs, something dark lurked.

She remembered her conversation with Jane the night before about unfinished business. What if they had all been summoned back to the ranch not so much for a reunion but for a reckoning?

Crazy thought. What reckoning? What had any of them done that had been so bad?

Ava admonished herself for her useless speculation as she retraced her steps along the trail. She needed to stay focused on her footing. The rain had started to come down harder and the smooth stones soon became slippery. She knew only one way out of the canyon and that was the way she'd come in. A good climber might have been able to scale the wall, using cracks and crevices for hand- and toeholds. That option wasn't available to Ava.

She didn't panic. The rain had only just started, and it would take a deluge for the canyon to fill up. But Ava had been caught in a flash flood in Houston once and the terror of all that rising water remained. It had happened so quickly, she and the other drivers had had to flee their cars and scramble for high ground. In a matter of moments, the downtown streets had become a vast waste- land of abandoned vehicles and rushing water.

The memory prodded her to the point of carelessness. She slipped and came down hard on one knee, and the jagged edge of a rock sliced into her flesh. The stinging pain, let alone the rivulets of blood down her shin, forced her to pause and take stock. She had just bent to examine the wound when a noise over the pounding rain froze her. She thought it was thunder at first. And indeed, she could hear lingering booms as the storm strengthened and rolled in. But the sound she heard now was directly over her.

The avalanche started with a cracking sound, followed by a shower of gravel. Ava glanced up, more curious than afraid, because the danger hadn't yet registered. She was still too focused on the storm. Something moved at the top of the canyon, a flash of yellow that she could barely discern through the rain-drops that clung to her lashes. And then the roar intensified as a boulder came tumbling down the face of the canyon.

The weight and momentum dislodged other stones, and Ava watched as the cliff seemed to crumble on top of her. Then her instincts kicked in and she scrambled from the path, tripping in her haste to avoiding the falling debris. Sharp pebbles pelted her skin before she managed to crawl beneath a narrow ledge.

Bruised and battered, she drew herself up, ducking her head and hugging her knees as she pressed herself against the wall. When the trembling subsided, she eased from un-derneath the shelter and stared in horrified wonder at the barricade that now blocked her way out of the canyon.

Still, she didn't panic. She could climb over

the rocks, she assured herself. The trail on the other side of the barrier would be clear. It was only a matter of time before she would be back at the ranch, sipping cocktails with Celeste.

No, she didn't panic. Not until she realized her phone had been crushed when she fell, and now she had no way of contacting the outside world.

"You're fine, you're fine," she muttered as she approached the precarious wall. She tried to pull herself up, but a stone shifted beneath her weight, and she realized the whole stack could come tumbling down upon her if she made even the slightest wrong move.

Best not to risk it, she decided. If she became pinned, she had no way to call for help. Nothing to do but turn around and head back the way she'd just come. There was bound to be another way out of the canyon.

DYLAN STOOD ON the patio, watching the rain. He and the others had decided to delay the climb as they'd watched the clouds roll in. Good call. The day had been sunny when they first set out that morning, but the sky had darkened quickly. Despite Jane's insistence that the storm was hours away, common sense prevailed among the other climbers, and she'd gone off in a huff. Everyone else had returned to the ranch. Celeste had headed down to the springs before the rain came, and Blair had disappeared upstairs after Tony had announced he was driving back to Austin for a business meeting. He would return sometime later that afternoon. Dylan had asked Blair if she wanted him to tail Tony back to the city, but she'd adamantly insisted that he stay and keep an eye on things at the ranch. For all either of them knew, she was now the target of her husband's business opposition, and she didn't want to be left unprotected.

Dylan agreed with her decision, but at the moment, Blair and Tony Redding had been pushed to the back of his mind. With each passing minute, he was getting more and more concerned about Ava. Where was she?

At first he'd just been annoyed that she'd gone off alone, but as the sky grew bleaker and the rain came down harder, his anger quickly morphed into uneasiness and then outright fear. He just wanted to find her.

Someone was coming across the property now. Dylan straightened, keeping his gaze fixed on the hurrying figure. Cloaked in a yellow rain slicker, Noah Pickett splashed across the yard to take refuge on the patio. He threw off the hood and shook raindrops from his poncho like a wet dog.

"Man, it's really coming down now," he said. "I moved my stuff down to one of the cabins. Figured I best keep an eye on the creek."

"You didn't see anyone else down that way, did you?"

Noah had been fiddling with the snaps on the slicker, but now he looked up sharply. "No, why?"

"Ava's missing. She wasn't inside when we got back from Bishop's Rock. No one has seen her since early this morning."

Something flashed in Noah's eyes before he glanced over his shoulder into the house. "Did you check with the staff? Maybe she said something to someone before she left."

"I tried, but most of the employees went home as soon as the weather service issued flash flood warnings for the area."

Noah nodded. "They have kids and family to consider. Can't afford to get stranded away from home overnight, much less indefinitely. I'm letting the rest go, too, so you all will have to fend for yourselves until the weather clears."

"Should we consider evacuating?" Dylan asked.

"No, you're better off here than out on the road. The freeway may already be closed in places. I'll go in and talk to the remaining staff. Maybe someone saw Ava leave."

"Thanks. I appreciate that."

"Try not to worry. We had a nice conversation on the way in from the airport. She struck me as someone with a good head on her shoulders. Maybe she's taken shelter somewhere to wait out the storm."

Dylan glanced at him. "Like where?"

Noah fell silent for a moment as he looked out over the grounds. "Lots of caves around here." His voice sounded oddly hushed, almost pained. "I know this place better than anyone and there are still places to hide I haven't yet found."

Worry burrowed deep inside Dylan's gut, and he couldn't shake a feeling of impending doom that had blown in with the storm.

"She can't have gone too far on foot," Noah said. "You tried her phone?"

"It went straight to voice mail," Dylan muttered.

Noah was right. Ava did have a good head on her shoulders. If she'd been able, she would have returned to the ranch before the storm hit. If she'd found shelter somewhere, she would have called.

Worry burrowed deeper and deeper.

He scanned the sky, looking for a break in the clouds. "I have a bad feeling about this."

Noah gave him a long scrutiny. "Where are the others?"

"Blair is upstairs. I'm not sure about Jane and Celeste. Why?"

"Just wanted to know if we should be looking for anyone else. Water can come up fast around here. Easy to get caught in a low spot."

"It hasn't been raining that long," Dylan said.

"Doesn't take long."

Dylan scanned the dreary landscape. "I'm going out to look for her."

"You sure that's a good idea? Might be best to wait it out. If the rain slacks, she'll probably make a run for it."

"I'm going," Dylan said.

"Then I'll go out with you. I'll round up whoever is left to help us. The more eyes out there, the better."

Dylan nodded. "We should start at the canyon. When we came here back in college, she always liked to look for fossils while the rest of us climbed."

Noah looked alarmed. "The canyon? That's the worst place to be in a flood."

"Then we shouldn't waste time," Dylan said.

"You'll find rain gear in the storage shed out back. Should be some waterproof flashlights, too."

They parted in the foyer, Noah to round up the remaining staff and Dylan to grab the flashlights. He didn't bother with the rain gear. Someone else had, though. One of the yellow slickers hung dripping from a hook in the corner.

THE RAIN CAME down so hard Ava could barely see in front of her. Like cats and dogs, her grandmother would say.

It was breathtaking and terrifying how quickly the landscape had transformed from a dry riverbed to a rushing stream. The water swirled about her ankles, not yet deep enough or strong enough to knock her off her feet, but the persistent tug made her escape more perilous. She had a vague hope that the rocks and boulders that had tumbled down the canyon to block her path might also work as a dam to slow the water until she could find another way out.

Drenched and shivering, she dug out her phone and tried once again to make a call or send a text, but the cracked screen was the least of the damage. She put the case back in her pocket and glanced at the sky, a dark, unyielding gray save for the lightning bolts that were followed by booming thunder. She watched the fireworks for a moment, and then plunged ahead despite her cut knee, despite the bruises from the falling rocks, despite the helplessness that was starting to gnaw at her resolve.

She cursed herself for being so stupid as to get caught at the bottom of a canyon in a rainstorm. Why hadn't she just gone with the others to Bishop's Rock? What was so great about being alone, anyway?

With an effort, she beat back her despondency. *Just keep your head down and keeping going*, she told herself firmly. *Find a way out or at least make it to high ground.*

The stream was up to her calves now, the current so strong she had trouble staying on her feet. The water was cold, too. Her teeth chattered and her fingers and toes had gone numb. She zipped up her jacket for all the protection it offered. The fabric was soaked. She was soaked. All she could think about was a hot bath. *Just keep going. Don't stop. One foot after the other.*

Exhaustion set in, followed by a dangerous lethargy. She just needed to rest for a minute. She was so tired, she could sit right down in the water, maybe even close her eyes for a bit.

She allowed herself a brief pause to scout for an outcropping or even a cave she could climb up to, but she doubted she could manage more than a few vertical feet in her current condition. If she tried to go higher and fell, turned an ankle or broke a leg…

Best not to dwell on worst-case scenarios. Surely someone at the ranch would be missing her by now. They would undoubtedly send out a search party when enough time had passed. But even if the whole place turned out to look for her, it could take hours in this weather. She was miles from the entrance to the canyon and a barricade of rocks blocked the trail. And as much as she might want to scream for help, the effort would be a useless waste of her energy. The din of the storm would drown her out.

Nothing to do but keep going...

The water rose to her knees. She was swept off her feet and carried downstream before she managed to find a handhold in the wall of the canyon. She clung to the slippery rock with her fingertips until the force of the current tore her loose. Then she was back in the water, battling time and Mother Nature as she gasped and sputtered for breath.

Surfacing, she grabbed for the wall in desperation. The rock slashed through the tender pads of her fingers, but she ignored the stinging pain as she gripped the side of the canyon. Bracing herself against the current, she inched forward. Little by little. *Just keep going.*

She lost all track of time. She didn't think she'd been gone more than a few hours, but the landscape was as dark as midnight. The water kept rising. Soon it would be up to her waist, up to her chest, up to her chin. Time and again, she was swept off her feet, buffeted against the canyon walls until she couldn't tell where one pain ended and another began. Winded and exhausted, she once more felt the seductive lure of letting go. *Just close your eyes and let it happen.*

Fingers caught in her hair, ripping wet strands from her scalp. Ava screamed in agony and tried to fight off her attacker, but she was so tired. So cold. *I can't...*

Yes, you can, Ava. You can fight as long as you have to. You hear me?

She wasn't sure, but she thought the voice in her head belonged to Dylan. Where was he? she wondered. Had he missed her yet? Would he come and find her when he realized she was in danger? Or did he even care anymore?

Don't do that. Don't feel sorry for yourself. Keep going, Ava. You can do this.

The fingers snatched another clump of hair from her scalp. Ava reached up to free herself, realizing almost instantly that her assailant was a dead tree that had fallen into the canyon and become wedged between the walls.

A lifeline...

Using a branch for leverage, she pulled herself up and onto the trunk. The tree wouldn't hold her forever. The force of rushing water would soon dislodge it from the walls, but for a moment, she had a respite, a chance to catch her breath and regroup. The water was too high now to walk out of the canyon. She was a strong swimmer but not in her physical condition and not in that current. The moment she let go of the tree trunk, she would be swept away, pummeled against those craggy walls as if she had no more substance than a rag doll. Her only way out was up.

She lifted her head to scan the rim of the canyon as raindrops battered her face. For a moment she thought she saw someone peering down at her, but it was nothing more than her imagination.

"Ava! Ava! Can you hear me?"

Dylan was inside her head again, calling her name.

"I can't hold on for much longer," she whispered.

"Ava!"

She lifted her head once more to the sound. Was he really there or had exhaustion played another cruel trick on her?

"Ava!"

"Dylan!" His name came out on a gasp. She drew a breath and tried again. "I'm down here! Can you see me? I'm trapped."

"I see you! Don't worry. I'll get you out. Just hold on, okay? I'm coming down."

"No, don't! There's no way out!"

"Just hold on!"

The tree moved a few inches and then wedged once more against the canyon walls. Ava wrapped her arms around a branch and held on for dear life as she peered through the rainy darkness. She prayed that Dylan would reach her in time and she prayed that he wouldn't even try. The canyon was a death trap. Even if he managed to find a way down, there was no way out. They would both be carried away. Already the tree was nearly submerged.

She gave a little cry as Dylan lowered himself over the edge of the canyon, pausing to find his footing and then clinging to the slippery rock as he climbed down the wall. Ava couldn't watch and yet she couldn't bear to look away. She'd seen him fall once. She wouldn't be able to stand it if she were the cause of a serious injury or worse.

On and on he came, slowly but surely, with nerves of steel. He lost his hold once and clung with one hand until he found another hold. When he neared the bottom of the canyon, he paused to scope out his surroundings and then inched his way horizontally across the wall to a narrow ledge. So near and yet so far away. Ava watched him breathlessly.

He fished a light from his bag, and she heard him call up to someone as he ran the beam over the tree until he found Ava.

"Are you hurt?" he called over the roar of rain and rushing water.

"No, I don't think so. Not seriously."

"Listen to me carefully. I'm going to toss you a rope. Put the loop around your body and hold on to the line as tight as you can. I'll do the rest."

"I can't let go. The current is too strong. I'll be swept away."

"Then I'll come to you."

"No, don't! It's too risky. Throw me the rope."

"Here it comes. Just grab it and hold on. Trust me, okay? I'll get you out."

Ava tried to position herself so that she would be ready, but the tree shifted with even the slightest movement. She held her breath and waited. It was difficult to see anything in the downpour. The rope swung by her and she missed it. The loop snagged on a branch, just out of her reach.

"Do you see it?" Dylan called.

"Yes. It's caught on a tree branch."

"Can you reach it?"

"I'll try."

"Be careful, Ava."

The way he said her name drew a shiver, not from cold or fear but from ten years of pent-up emotion. A decade of denying her true feelings. If she got out of this alive, if they both made it back to the ranch in one piece…

Don't think about that now. Just get to the rope.

She tried to ease along the trunk, but that didn't work, so she lowered herself into the water. The current took her by surprise and she almost lost her grip. Clinging to a branch with one hand, she tugged at the rope, but that only tightened the loop. Taking a deep breath, she plunged underwater, using the submerged limbs to propel her body forward and then up. The movement freed the tree and the current swung the trunk around, hitting her with enough force to knock her back against the wall. She went under again, caught in a tangle of branches.

Limbs caught in her clothing, pulling her deeper underwater. She thrashed frantically, releasing a frenzy of bubbles as she tried to free herself. Tearing her arms free of the caught jacket, she surfaced and gasped for air, too exhausted and frightened to think straight. Yet somehow she'd managed to hang on to the rope.

"Ava!"

"I'm okay! I got it!" She pulled the rope over her head and under her arms, grasping the line for all she was worth as Dylan somehow managed to pull her toward him.

Later, she would learn that Noah and one of his coworkers had fastened a rope tightly to a boulder at the top of the canyon and lowered it down to Dylan so that he could anchor himself against the drag of her weight and the force of the current. But the rescue itself was a blur. The next thing she knew, she was out of the water and on the ledge with Dylan. And then she was being pulled upward in a makeshift sling, somehow managing to push off with her legs so that she wouldn't be smashed against the wall. A little while later, she was back at the ranch, back in her room, luxuriating in a steamy bath with no worry beyond keeping her bandaged knee dry and elevated on the side of the tub.

It wasn't until she was toweling her hair that she remembered that curious flash of yellow a split second before the canyon wall had caved in on her.

Chapter Seven

By late afternoon, the yard was one big puddle and the ditches had overflowed onto the driveway. The house remained high and dry, but the road was a different matter. After Dylan had seen Ava settled at the ranch, he'd walked out to the highway to survey the damage. For as far as he could see in every direction, nothing but water, deep enough to strand even a four-wheel-drive vehicle. The only way in and out of Whispering Springs was by boat or helicopter, but the isolation wasn't necessarily a bad thing from his perspective. No one could leave the ranch, but no one was likely to show up without his knowing, either.

However, they weren't completely cut off. His cell phone was still working. He placed a call to his people in Houston and another to the nearest law enforcement office to alert them of the situation. Nothing more to be done except to sit tight and stay alert.

He left the highway and walked all the way down to the creek. The normally slow and meandering waterway had turned into a raging river. He stood at the top of the ravine, gazing down in amazement as trees, debris and even a car swept by. Thankfully no one was inside the vehicle, and Dylan could only hope the driver and any passengers had made it to high ground without injury. The ease with which the water carried away an automobile was a testament to the ferocity and speed of the storm.

When Dylan got back to the house, the downstairs was deserted. Noah had sent the rest of the staff home right after the rescue and everyone else had gone up to their rooms. Ava's close call had shaken the group, and Dylan doubted anyone would be foolish enough to venture out for the rest of the day.

He completed his rounds and then headed up to his room for a quick shower and dry clothes. Then he went next door to check on Ava. She answered his knock in her bathrobe, looking both ways down the corridor before stepping back to allow him to enter.

He took in the scrapes and bruises on her face as he stepped across the threshold. But her demeanor, more than her injuries, caught his attention. She seemed nervous to the point of frightened. He knew from experience that once the adrenaline rush subsided, shock could set in.

"You okay?"

"I'm still a little on edge," she admitted as she closed the door and then hugged her arms to her middle. "But I'll live, thanks to you."

"How's the knee? That cut looked deep enough to need stitches."

"Blair brought up bandages and antiseptic. It wasn't so bad once we got it cleaned up. Good thing, too." She waved an arm toward the open balcony doors. Outside the rain had slacked to a drizzle, but Dylan could hear the rumble of thunder in the distance as another storm approached. "I don't think a trip to the ER is in my near future, do you?"

"Probably not. I've been out checking the roads. Unless it's an extreme emergency, I'd say we're stuck here for at least another forty-eight hours. Search and rescue teams already have their hands full and it's bound to get worse if the water keeps rising."

"Two more days." She walked over to the open doorway to stare out. "You know what's funny?" she said with her back to him. "I'd planned to stay until the weekend anyway, but being stranded here is different. It makes me claustrophobic. Another day of this and I'll be climbing the walls. I should have checked the weather before I came."

"No one could have predicted anything like this." Dylan followed her across the room, leaning a shoulder against the door frame as he eyed the gray sky. "The storm moved in quickly and caught us all by surprise."

"At least the rest of you were smart enough to avoid the canyon. I can't believe I let myself get caught down there in a flash flood."

"Don't beat yourself up," he said. "If we hadn't planned a climb, any one of us could have been down there with you."

"I guess."

"Just try to relax. Nothing we can do but wait it out."

"Easier said than done."

"I did say 'try.'"

A smile flitted before she turned back to

scan the watery landscape. "Do you really think we're safe here?"

"I talked to Noah earlier. The ranch has a backup generator and there's plenty of food and bottled water to last for days. We should be fine."

She gave him a sidelong glance. "I wasn't talking about the floodwaters."

"What's going on, Ava?"

She hesitated. "I don't know. It may be nothing."

"Tell me anyway."

She slipped her hands into the pockets of her robe and hunched her shoulders, as if she were trying to seek refuge inside the soft fabric. "It happened right before the rock slide. I heard a noise and when I looked up, I saw something yellow at the top of the canyon. I only caught a glimpse," she was quick to explain. "And I'm still not sure of what I actually saw."

Dylan found himself flashing back to the bottom of the canyon, to the tremble of her body as he pulled her from the rushing water and the thud of her heart as he held her close. *I'm okay, I'm okay*, she'd whispered over and over until he finally remembered that he had a job to do. He'd released her then, turning away abruptly to attend to the final stage of the rescue. When she finally disappeared over the rim of the canyon to safety, the emotions that washed over him had been so unexpected and so intense he'd been glad to have a few minutes alone to collect his cool before his ascent up the canyon wall.

He gave her a quizzical look. "That's it? You glimpsed something yellow at the top of the canyon?"

"I didn't have time to think about it then. I was too busy dodging boulders. It was only later, when I got back to the ranch and I could catch my breath, that I remembered it at all. I think what I saw was a rain slicker."

Dylan straightened, an uneasy thrill chasing down his spine. "You're sure it wasn't Noah or one of the other rescuers?"

"The rock slide happened a long time before you came along. It seemed like hours."

"You never saw a face or heard a voice? Think hard."

She made an impatient gesture. "I've been thinking of little else all afternoon. I know it's not much to go on and to be perfectly honest, it may have been nothing more than my imagination. I was already uneasy and it was raining so hard I could barely see my hand in front of me, let alone all the way to the top of the canyon. But I can't dismiss the possibility that someone was up there."

He said slowly, "Do you think this person started the rock slide?"

She seemed to huddle even more deeply inside her robe. "I don't know. I haven't wanted to take it that far."

"I think we have to," he said. "Let's just start with a basic question. Do you know of anyone who would want to hurt you?"

She shot him a glance. "At any given time? Probably a dozen or more inmates at the Harris County Jail. You don't work in the DA's office for as long as I have without making enemies. But do I think someone *here* has it in for me? No, of course not. And yet…"

"You saw something."

"I saw something."

"Any theories?"

"Not really," she said with a shrug. "Maybe it was just a random stranger. A climber or a hiker who got caught out in the storm as I did. Maybe they didn't even see me in the canyon. That's the most likely explanation."

"But?"

She watched the rain with a brooding scowl. "Ever since that doll turned up in Blair's room, I've had a bad feeling about all of us being together again. I can buy the threatening phone calls and even the break-in as corporate dirty tricks, but I still say that broken doll felt personal. Like someone is using the reunion to send us a message. Call it a premonition or intuition or plain old gut instinct, but I know you sense it, too."

Yes, he'd sensed it, but the feeling was so nebulous he was hard-pressed to explain it. He'd experienced it on the roof last night and again today as he walked the flooded property. It was nothing concrete, just a nagging worry that something wasn't right. That he had been brought to Whispering Springs for a darker purpose. Maybe they all had.

"I keep going back to a conversation I had with Jane last night," Ava said.

"What about?"

"Apparently she thinks we never properly dealt with Lily's suicide. According to her, we swept our guilt under the rug and got on with our lives as if nothing had happened. As if Lily never mattered. But it wasn't so much what Jane said as her behavior. You should have seen her, Dylan. She had this look in her eyes. It made me think of something you once told me in college about her friendship with Lily. You thought she was clingy, remember? You said her behavior was possessive and creepy. That was a very specific observation and it made an impact. I could never look at her in quite the same way again."

He conjured an image of Jane Sandoval then and now. She had always been different. Withdrawn and resentful with an intensity bordering on obsession. From their brief interaction at the ranch, he didn't think she'd changed much over the years, although she had certainly been professionally successful. A basic background check had revealed a rapid climb up the corporate ladder at the Austin tech firm where she worked. For a while, Dylan had considered her a person of interest in the Tony Redding case, but a more comprehensive investigation of her company had turned up no apparent affiliation or interface with Redding Technologies and the impending merger.

Still, in light of what Ava had just told him, Dylan decided Jane Sandoval's history warranted closer scrutiny. At the very least, she was someone worth keeping an eye on.

Maybe Ava was right, he thought. The phone calls and break-in and especially the mutilated doll left on Blair's bed might have nothing to do with Tony Redding's business and everything to do with a personal griev-ance. Someone might be trying to rattle a few cages.

He scrubbed a hand down the side of his face. "Do you think it's possible Jane has been harboring a grudge all these years on Lily's behalf?"

"As I said, I haven't wanted to take it that far, but she makes no bones about her disdain for us. And she seems to have an obsessive personality. I don't know why I never saw it before. You certainly had her pegged. I just thought she was a little needy. But I've re-membered other things…other conversations that trouble me."

Dylan glanced at her. "What conversa-tions?"

"Jane was all set to attend graduate school in Austin, and then she changed her mind at the last minute and accepted a job offer in California. Maybe there was nothing suspicious about her decision. Maybe she just needed to get away. We all scattered that summer."

Was that an accusatory note he heard in her tone? Dylan let it go, determined to stay focused. "You think there was something else behind her sudden change of heart?"

"I don't know, but she never even mentioned a job offer until she was already packed and ready to leave. It was like she couldn't wait to get out of town. I'm the one who drove her to the airport. That day, she seemed consumed by the more gruesome aspects of Lily's last moments—who and what had been on her mind, if she'd felt any pain. That kind of thing. I guess it's only natural to brood about a tragedy. To fret over what might have been done differently. I certainly did enough of that after Lily died. But even then, as upset as we both were, there was something about Jane's fixation that bothered me."

"You never said anything."

"How could I? You'd already gone away yourself by that time. I didn't say anything to the others because I thought Jane might be right. Maybe I did want to sweep my feelings under a rug and get on with my life. But if you could have heard her last night on the patio, the way she talked about this place and about us, she almost sounded unbalanced."

"That's a very serious charge, Ava."

"I know, and I don't make it lightly. But believe me, I've seen unbalanced. I've seen obsession."

Dylan thought about all those write-ups in the paper extolling Ava's fierce dedication and her willingness, even fervor, to prosecute cases no one else wanted to touch.

"You've probably seen a little of everything in your line of work," he offered.

Her shudder was almost imperceptible. "You've no idea. Which is why Jane's behavior last night set off my alarm. She talked about a girl who vanished from Whispering Springs a few years back. Noah mentioned the disappearance on the way here from the airport so he probably told Jane about her, too. According to him, this girl went out to walk the trails one evening and never came back. Jane implied that something supernatural had happened to her."

A feeling of foreboding descended as Dylan searched the early twilight. He didn't believe in the supernatural. He'd never seen evidence of ghosts or goblins or things that went bump in the night, but he'd encountered darkness. He'd seen evil up close and personal in ravaged villages and along the mined roadsides of Afghanistan. He experienced an inkling of that malevolence now, though he told himself he was letting the weather and Ava's misgivings get to him.

He tried to put a more palatable face on her qualms. "Are you sure Jane wasn't just pulling your leg? Back in the day, we all tried to outdo each other with our stories."

"I know. And I do think she was trying to get a rise out of me. But you said yourself she's always been a hard one to figure out. Do you even remember how she became a part of our group?"

"I always thought you brought her in."

"Me? No, it was Lily. Or maybe Blair. It's odd, isn't it? That we can't quite remember how or when Jane became one of us? She was just there one day and none of us questioned her presence. I do know one thing. There's no love lost between her and Celeste."

"Celeste seems to have a knack for getting under people's skin."

Ava turned in surprise. "Why do you say that?"

Dylan hesitated. "Because I saw something, too."

THE RAIN STARTED to come down harder, the drumming on the roof an echo of Ava's accelerated heartbeat. Dylan stared out at the downpour with a brooding scowl, seemingly oblivious to her scrutiny. She slid her gaze over his features as memories stirred. Strange that after all these years, he could still evoke a mixture of desire and melancholy.

"What did you see?" she pressed.

He gave her an uneasy glance. "We'll get to that. I need to ask you something first. Have you kept in touch with Celeste over the years? Do you know anything about her life in New Orleans?"

Ava frowned. "Not really. Early on, she and Blair and I would meet for the occasional weekend getaway. It was fine at first, but as time went on, we had nothing in common. The meetings became awkward and forced and we finally stopped making the effort. Celeste would still reach out now and then, but even her phone calls eventually fizzled."

Dylan was quiet for a moment. He seemed to choose his words carefully. "Did she ever confide in you?"

"About what?"

"Her personal life, business troubles. Anything."

The back of Ava's neck tingled a warning. "Why do I get the feeling you're fishing for something specific? What is it you really want to know?"

"I have to be careful what I say here." He lowered his voice as if to emphasize the need for discretion. "This is a sensitive matter and I haven't spoken to Blair yet. She's still my client."

"I understand you have a professional obligation to Blair. As I told you last night, I appreciate your ethics and your dilemma. But, Dylan, we both have an obligation to figure out what's going on before someone gets hurt." A hint of urgency crept into her tone. "Even if we dismiss what I saw at the top of the canyon, there's still the matter of that doll on Blair's bed and the threats to Tony. If a dangerous element has invaded Whispering Springs, we need to have each other's backs. We're cut off from the outside world until the water recedes. If there's more trouble, we can't expect the cavalry to come riding in. It's just you and me."

He gave her an assessing look. "What about the others?"

"I don't know them anymore and I don't trust them," she said bluntly.

"You don't know me, either. Ten years is a long time. People change."

She allowed a fleeting smile. "Not you. I don't believe it. You wouldn't have risked your life climbing down the wall of that canyon in the middle of a storm if you weren't still the Dylan Burkhart I once knew."

"Don't turn that into something it isn't. Anyone would have done the same."

She lifted a shoulder. "Maybe, maybe not. But you didn't hesitate." She let her head fall back against the door frame as she watched him. He seemed discomfited by her observation, and for some reason that amused her. "You always were a Boy Scout."

"A Boy Scout? That's what you thought of me?" The corners of his mouth twitched.

"With badass tendencies, but a Boy Scout nonetheless. I suspect the only difference now is that it's the other way around. The point I'm trying to make is this—I'm a good judge of character because I've had to be. My instinct is still to trust you, and whether you believe it or not, you can trust me, too."

He rubbed his forehead as if a headache had started to throb. "All right," he said. "But anything we discuss stays between us."

"Of course. Goes without saying."

"Celeste left her room last night to meet Tony Redding."

Ava straightened in shock. "Tony? Are you sure?"

"I saw them together."

"*Together* together?"

"Not in the way you mean. I spotted his car at the end of the driveway. He'd pulled to the side of the road so that he could park in the shadows. When Celeste left the house, he flashed his lights to let her know he was there. Then the two of them got into an altercation."

"What kind of altercation?"

"I couldn't hear their conversation, but I saw Tony get out of the car and grab her arm. Celeste tried to slap him and they scuffled. By the time I arrived, Tony had climbed back into his car. He drove to the ranch and Celeste followed on foot."

Ava took a moment to digest his revelation. Tony and Celeste. How long had *that* been going on?

"Did they see you?" she asked anxiously.

"No. I kept to the shadows, too. But I got the impression it was anything but a random confrontation. Something is going on between those two."

"An affair?"

He shrugged. "Or a bad breakup, maybe. Tony was never the type of guy to take no for an answer."

Ava leaned back against the door frame again as she thought about the implications. "This is all very sordid, isn't it? I guess I never realized how incestuous our group is. Or maybe I did. Maybe that's why I could never accept us as a couple."

Something flashed in Dylan's eyes, but his voice remained calm. "You and I did nothing wrong. But you did your damnedest to make it seem as though we had."

She sighed. "I suppose it was easier that way."

"Easier how?" he demanded.

"Easier to break things off with you out of guilt than to admit to myself that I was afraid."

That stopped him cold. "Of me?"

"No, not of you. Not physically. It was all just so intense." She paused, wondering why she felt compelled to explain herself after all these years. Couples broke up all the time. Love affairs came to an end. How could any of this possibly matter now? And yet the words tumbled out unabridged as if the truth could somehow redeem her in Dylan's eyes. She refused to speculate on why his opinion still mattered so much. "I don't do relationships. I just don't. There's something missing in me, I think."

His skeptical silence said it all. He wasn't going to make it easy for her.

"That sounds dramatic and self-indulgent, but I don't know how else to explain it. My parents just celebrated their fortieth wedding anniversary and both sets of my grandparents were together forever. My sister is happily married and my brother is in a committed relationship, and then there's me. As soon as I start getting close to someone, I pull back. I break things off. I turn tail and run."

Dylan studied her for a moment. "You couldn't have just told me that?"

"I don't think I even realized it at the time. It's taken a lot of years of self-reflection to figure it out. Not that I still completely understand it. I just thought you should know." She leaned her cheek against the rough wood. "It was never about you and only a little about Lily. It was me."

"Why are you telling me this now?" He didn't sound angry, just mildly annoyed.

Ava couldn't help feeling a little dejected by his response. Whatever she'd expected, his bemused expression wasn't it. "Just clearing the air, I guess."

He said nothing else, and they turned as one to watch the rain. The landscape looked bleak and formidable, the ranch a drowned, dreary outpost. *What a lonely place this is*, Ava thought as she wandered through her memories.

Ten years had gone by since last she'd seen

Dylan and she was still trying to make sense of why she'd sent him away. One moment, one decision and two lives had been irrevocably changed. Regret had never tasted so bitter.

She felt his gaze on her and mustered a smile. "I didn't mean to wade so deeply into our past. I've always been an overanalyzer and I hate leaving things unfinished. Everything needs to fit in a neat compartment before I can put it away. I guess it's the lawyer in me."

Dylan didn't return her smile. "For what it's worth, I realized pretty quickly you'd done the right thing."

An irrational hurt curled up in her chest. "Oh?"

"I had a lot of growing up to do back then. Everything had always come too easy for me. School, sports, Lily. I needed someone to throw me a curveball."

"Dylan, you lost both your parents when you were just fifteen. How was that easy?"

"It was devastating," he agreed. "But I had a grandmother who took me in and cared for me as if I were her own. I couldn't have asked for a better home. I never wanted for anything until you came along."

Anger pricked at Ava's poise. "I throw you one curveball and you run off to join the military?"

"I didn't run off. The decision was anything but rash. It was something I'd been thinking about for a long time."

"You never told me."

He did smile then. "We didn't do a lot of talking back then."

Just like that, Ava's anger faded and she felt the impact of that smile all the way to her toes.

"Not that it matters now," he added.

"Right." She lifted her face to the darkening sky, watching the distant flicker of lightning as she battled a lingering gloom. "Life can be so strange. After all these years, after serving your country on the other side of the world, you end up in Houston. In my city. I still can't believe our paths never crossed. Maybe that should tell us something."

"That we were never meant to be? I wouldn't put too much trust in fate if I were you. Our paths did cross once. Twice, actually."

She turned in surprise. "When was this?"

"A month or so after I moved to Houston.

I saw you in a restaurant. For about two seconds, I considered coming over to say hello, and then thought better of it. I wasn't sure of my reception. Plus, it seemed like you were involved in a pretty intense conversation and I didn't want to bother you. A few days later I drove by your apartment."

"How did you know where I lived?"

"It's not hard to find an address in my line of work."

"Apparently not. Wow." She shook her head in disbelief. "I don't even know what to say to that."

"It only happened the one time. You don't need to worry that I've been stalking you."

She laughed softly. "I'm not at all worried. Honestly, had I known you were in town I probably would have done the same to you. It's human nature to be curious."

"Thank you for that."

She gave him a look. "It's not like I haven't thought about you over the years. It's not like I haven't wondered where you were and what you were doing. If you still remembered me."

"I told you before, I remember everything."

Damn, but he knew how to get to her.

She tucked back her hair, surprised to find

a weakness in her fingers. "Why did you really come to my room, Dylan?"

"I wanted to make sure you were all right."

"And now?"

"I've been standing here asking myself that same question. I don't know why I'm still here. I don't know why we're doing this dance."

"Don't you?" She placed a tentative hand on his arm.

"This isn't a good idea, Ava."

She closed her eyes on a shiver. "I always loved the way you said my name." She reached up and trailed a knuckle down his cheek. He caught her hand and for a moment they froze, gazes locked. Ava's pulse was suddenly racing and she felt breathless and confused. How could the years fall away so easily? In the space of a heartbeat, she was back in college, back in love, back in Dylan Burkhart's arms.

"Ava." A whisper. An admonishment.

"It's okay."

"You don't really want to do this." His eyes glinted in the murky light. "Aside from the obvious pitfalls, reunion hookups are cliché as hell."

"Maybe *cliché* just means *uncomplicated.*"

He lifted his gaze skyward. "You, me, sex. That's the very definition of *complicated.*"

"It doesn't have to be." Ava told herself to accept his resistance and move on. But she couldn't help herself. She wanted him. Maybe it was the isolation of the ranch or her harrowing experience in the canyon that made her crave affirmation and human companionship. Or maybe it had just been too long since she'd been in the company of a man who truly intrigued her. A man who could turn her on with just a lingering look or the flicker of a smile. Or the way he said her name. "We're both adults, Dylan. Where's the harm so long as we both realize it's just a one-time thing?"

"A one-time thing." He looked amused. "You really think I'm that kind of guy? I'm a Boy Scout, remember?"

"With badass tendencies. Don't forget that part."

His smiled vanished as he wrapped an arm around her waist and drew her to him. "It's been a long time, Ava."

"Don't I know it?" She fought the urge to melt into him. Instead, she pressed her palms to his chest, putting up walls even as she urged him to surrender.

"I didn't come to your room with expectations" he seemed compelled to add.

"I know. And I didn't come to Whispering Springs with any, either. But here we are."

She rose on tiptoe, lifting her face to his kiss. He threaded his fingers through her hair, tasting her gingerly at first and then with growing heat as she pulled him back toward the bed.

"Just like that?" he murmured against her mouth.

"Just like that." She fell against the pillows and tugged him down with her.

He lifted himself off her. "You're all banged up. I don't want to hurt you."

"You let me worry about that. Just take off your shirt."

He removed his weapon first, placing it on the nightstand, and then he whipped the shirt over his head and tossed it aside. Ava splayed her hands on his chest, running her fingers admiringly over the hard muscles in his shoulders and arms.

Her breath sharpened. "How do you do that?"

"Do what?"

"This." She traced his abs. "You don't even look real. No one should be that perfect."

"That doesn't sound like much of a compliment."

"Then you obviously haven't checked yourself out in the mirror lately."

"Take off your robe."

She pulled it more tightly around her. "No way. I'm too intimidated now."

"You've *never* been intimidated," he said as he fumbled with the ties, shoving the fabric aside to expose every inch of her body to his gleaming eyes.

He kissed her again, positioning himself on his side as he cupped one breast and then the other. Trailing his hand down her abdomen, he lingered between her thighs until her pulse quickened and she grew flushed.

"Now the pants," she whispered as she flattened her hand across his zipper.

"I'd forgotten how bossy you are." He got up to remove the rest of his clothing.

She propped herself on one elbow to watch him. "I prefer *assertive*."

"You're assertively staring."

"I know."

He climbed back into bed, wrapping a leg

over her as he pulled her close. "So…we're really doing this," he murmured.

"We're really doing this."

"Ava—"

She put a fingertip to his lips. "No more talk."

"Fine by me."

They kissed, again and again, and then he nudged apart her legs, teasing with his fingers and then with his tongue until they were both hot and ready.

"In the nightstand," she breathed. "Courtesy of management."

"That was thoughtful."

"And a bit optimistic, but yes. Very thoughtful."

She lay on top of him, kissing and teasing him. It was all playful and uncomplicated until Dylan rolled her on her back and stared down at her for the longest moment, his gaze dark and hooded. Memories stirred once more and Ava found herself thinking about the past, about their first time, about how deeply in love they'd once been. And how everything had gone so wrong.

That was a long time ago, she reminded herself. It didn't have to be like that now.

They were both older and wiser, hopefully a little more sophisticated. Sex didn't have to mean anything. It could just be about this one time, this one moment...

She plunged her fingers in his hair, arching her hips to meet his and then wrapping her legs around him so tightly no daylight showed between them.

On and on they moved until their bodies were straining and shuddering and they were both gasping for breath.

Chapter Eight

Ava rested her cheek on Dylan's shoulder as she listened to the rain. The drumbeat against the windows no longer seemed gloomy but cozy. The unease she'd experienced earlier would eventually return, but for now she felt lazy and content, with no greater ambition than to snuggle under the covers with an old lover. "It's still coming down hard out there," she murmured.

His arm tightened around her. "We'll be okay. But I need to get up and take another look around the property. I still have a job to do."

"Give me a minute and I'll come with you. I'm too comfortable to move right now."

He dropped a kiss in her hair. "Stay put. I'll make the rounds."

"We're supposed to watch out for each other, remember? I was serious about that."

"I know you were. But there's no point in both of us going out in this weather. Someone needs to keep an eye on things inside."

Ava teased circles on his chest with her fingertip. "What do you think the others are doing right now?"

"Staying out of trouble, I hope. I'm counting on the rain to keep everyone inside for the rest of the day."

"There's no one here besides our group. Blair said the staff left as soon as the flooding started."

"My concern is that someone arrived before the roads became impassable and now they're trapped here with us."

"All the more reason we need to stick together." Ava slipped from the crook of his arm and rolled to her back as disquiet returned. "Why do you think Tony left so suddenly? What could have been so urgent that he'd leave Blair here after everything that's happened? Do you think she told him about the doll?"

"Could we not talk about this right now?" He propped his hands behind his head as he stared at the ceiling. "Blair is still my client.

I need to discuss certain things with her before I keep talking to you about it."

"You didn't have a problem earlier with our discussion."

"Ava."

"Okay, I get it." She tried not to take his rebuff personally. She knew about privilege and professional responsibility. In Dylan's place, she would be just as hesitant and wary. But the subtle distance he had created stung a little, which made no sense. Wasn't this what she wanted? No strings, no complications, a one-time-only thing? Normally she was the one throwing up barriers as she gathered her clothes and headed for the door. Served her right, she supposed, that Dylan was giving her a taste of her own medicine.

"Can I say just one more thing?"

He slanted her a cautious glance. "What is it?"

She slid her hand over his and squeezed. "It's not lost on me what you did today. The risk you took. You could have been killed trying to save my life."

"But I wasn't. We're both fine. Relatively speaking." His gaze slipped over her scrapes and bruises. "You would have done the same for me."

"I would have tried, but we both know I could never have climbed down that canyon wall."

"Then you would have found another way. Don't you remember what you did when you saw me fall that day? You were halfway up Bishop's Rock before I could give you the all-clear sign."

"Halfway up is a gross exaggeration, and as I recall, you had a devil of a time getting me back down. Don't equate one incident with the other. There's only one hero in this room."

He gave her a scowling glance. "I'm no hero."

"Army ranger, three combat tours, a Silver Star? That's about as heroic as you can get in my book." She smiled again at his discomfort. "Blair told me earlier about your record. To say that you were in the service for a time doesn't do justice to your sacrifice. You make the rest of us look like slackers."

"That's not true. There's more than one way to serve your country. What you do is important."

"Maybe. I used to think so." Ava paused,

plucking idly at the covers. "Do you know why I came to this reunion? I had to get out of town because I threw a temper tantrum in court. I diminished my standing and embarrassed my boss. He threatened to suspend me if I didn't make myself scarce for a week. I came here because I was afraid of what I'd do if I remained in Houston. Blair had already made all the arrangements so I took the path of least resistance."

Dylan turned. "Is this a confession or are you making a point?"

"I honestly don't know. Maybe I just needed a sympathetic ear. Or maybe I'm only now realizing that taking the path of least resistance has been my MO for a very long time."

He was silent for a moment. "You seem to think you owe me an explanation. You don't. The past is past. It's like you said earlier. None of this has to be complicated."

"That is what I said."

He rolled to his side, threading his fingers through her hair as he stared down at her. "Maybe you need to accept that some things are never going to fit in those neat compartments of yours. Life doesn't work that way."

"I'm starting to realize that, too."

He kissed her then, pulling her close for only a moment before he broke away. "I have to go."

"I know. Go do your thing."

He swung his legs over the side of the bed and reached for his clothes. When he came out of the bathroom a few minutes later, Ava was already dressed and back at the open balcony doors, staring out at the downpour. It was still early, but already twilight had deepened to nightfall. Without the stars and moon, the landscape looked eerie and forbidding. She could barely make out the silhouette of Bishop's Rock, let alone anything smaller. If a mere mortal roamed the soggy grounds, the darkness would cover his tracks.

She drew her sweater around her and hugged her arms to her middle as she turned back to Dylan.

"You okay?" he asked as he sat down on the edge of the bed to put on his shoes.

"Of course. Why wouldn't I be?"

"You seem to spend an inordinate amount of time staring out that window."

"I was just thinking. We don't have to talk about it now, but I meant what I said earlier. We need to figure out what's going on here before someone gets hurt. I have a bad feeling about all this, Dylan. Something is happening that we don't yet understand. It could be that I'm being overly cautious or overly imaginative, but I've learned to listen to my instincts."

"I agree, but we have to be discreet. We don't want to cause undue panic in the others or tip our hand too early to the perpetrator." He reached for his weapon on the nightstand and tucked it in the back of his jeans. "Keep your eyes and ears open, but no asking a lot of questions, okay?"

"Contrary to my recent meltdown, I know how to be subtle when the situation warrants."

"I didn't mean to offend you."

"You didn't. And your point is taken. We need to be careful."

"In everything we do. Use the dead bolt when you come in and make sure the balcony door is locked when you leave the room."

She shivered at his ominous tone. "Now you're making me uneasy."

"Good. I want you to be uneasy. You'll be more inclined to keep up your guard."

"You be careful, too," she said. "Dylan..."

Whatever she'd been about to say froze on

her lips as a muffled scream penetrated the walls. Their gazes held for only a second before Dylan lunged for the door. "Wait here," he said over his shoulder. But she was already at his heels.

THE DOOR ACROSS the hall opened and Blair came out. She looked as if she'd been sleeping—eyes bleary, clothing all rumpled. Tucking back her mussed hair, she blinked in their direction as if trying to focus. "I was napping and something woke me up. It sounded like a scream...or was I dreaming?"

"You weren't dreaming," Ava said. "We heard it, too."

"Stay in your room and lock the door," Dylan instructed, but Blair had already fallen into step behind him.

Ava glanced at her worriedly. "You okay?"

"I'm just a little groggy." She gave herself a shake as if to throw off a lingering lethargy, but she seemed so out of it that Ava wondered if she'd taken something. "What happened?" she asked as she rubbed a hand across her eyes.

"We don't know yet. Maybe you should go back inside your room," Ava suggested.

Dylan gave them both a look over his shoulder as if to say, *Enough with the chit-chat.*

Blair tucked her arm through Ava's and shivered. "What on earth is going on around this place? This is not at all the week I had planned."

"I know. Just stay close, okay?"

As they approached the end of the hallway, Celeste's door opened and she stuck her head out. In contrast to Blair's sluggishness, she seemed hyper. "What's going on?"

"That's what we're trying to find out," Dylan said in a low voice. "All of you, please, just go back to your rooms and lock your doors. I'll tell you when it's safe to come out."

"And let you have all the fun? Please. This is the most excitement we've had around here all day. With the exception of Ava's little adventure." Celeste pulled her door closed and moved into the hallway. Her gaze narrowed as she took in Dylan's untucked shirt and Ava's bare feet. She lifted one brow ever so slightly at Ava before turning back to Dylan. "Sounded like it came from Jane's room."

"I think so, too," Blair said as she clutched Ava's arm. "I hope she's okay. What should we do? Should we call down for a key?"

"Dylan could always kick in the door," Celeste suggested. She seemed to relish the prospect.

"Everybody, just calm down," he said in exasperation. "How about I try knocking first?" He moved across the hallway and rapped on Jane's door. "Jane, it's Dylan Burkhart. Everything okay in there?"

There was a moment of silence, followed by a frenzy of swearing, and then the door swung open and Jane stepped across the threshold, eyes blazing. Her hair was wet and spiky, and splotches of red colored her normally pale cheeks. She clenched her hands tightly at her sides as if she had to restrain herself from punching a wall. Or someone.

"Jane?" Ava said in concern. "Are you all right?"

"Do I look all right?"

"You look ready to explode," Celeste said a little too gleefully.

"I go out for some air and I come back

to *this*." Jane glanced over her shoulder into her room.

"What is *this*?" Dylan asked. "What happened?"

She blocked the doorway as her gaze zeroed in on Celeste. "Ask *her*."

Celeste frowned. "Ask me what?"

Jane's knuckles whitened, a dead giveaway to her highly agitated state. "You did this, Celeste. Don't even bother to deny it. I didn't tell anyone I was going out, but you're right across the hall. You must have heard me leave."

Celeste glanced around. "I'm sorry. Does anyone have a clue what she's babbling about?"

"Stop lying!" Jane lunged into the hallway, forcing Dylan to position himself between the two women in order to restrain her.

"Good grief, Jane. Calm down." Celeste brushed a hand down her sleeve as if soothing her own ruffled feathers.

Jane backed down physically but her eyes shot daggers across the hallway.

Dylan said in a placating tone, "Tell us what happened, Jane."

"She came into my room while I was out.

I know it was her because I smelled her disgusting perfume the minute I opened the door."

"Oh, for God's sake, I'm not even wearing perfume." Celeste held out her wrist. "Care to take a whiff?"

Jane said sullenly, "You probably showered and changed after you left."

"Right. I spritzed myself with perfume *before* I came to your room." Celeste cocked her head with a puzzled frown. "Now tell me again *why* I was there? And how I got in?"

"I left my door unlocked. You obviously just waltzed right in."

"You're delusional," Celeste said with a dismissive wave of her hand.

"Time-out," Dylan said with a menacing scowl. "Both of you, settle down so we can get to the bottom of this."

Ava stepped forward. "He's right. Let's all take a breath and calm down. Jane, tell us what happened. What's got you so upset?"

She pushed back wet strings of hair from her face. "As if any of you really give a damn."

Celeste leaned a shoulder against the wall and rolled her eyes.

"Of course we care," Ava said. "Just tell us what happened."

Jane stood back and motioned them inside. "Why don't you all come in and see for yourselves?"

"Finally," Celeste muttered.

Dylan took the lead, and Ava followed him through the door and down the narrow entrance hall into the bedroom. He didn't outwardly react to the discovery, but she sensed his tension a split second before she spotted the doll lying atop Jane's neatly made bed.

Like the one they'd found in Blair's room, the doll's limbs had been mangled and the head twisted to face the entrance. Light reflected from glassy eyes, creating the impression of life. The doll seemed to watch them.

Icy fingers tripped along Ava's spine. She wanted to break contact with that frozen glare, but there were too many details she needed to absorb. This doll was no collector's item, but a cheap vinyl toy that could have been purchased from any discount store. The clothing was caked with mud, the dark hair wet and crudely chopped off to resemble Jane's pixie cut. That alone gave Ava pause, but there was yet another difference. A red gash ran from ear to ear, deep enough to all but sever the plastic head.

Ava drew a sharp breath and reminded herself that a maimed doll was hardly the most disturbing thing she'd ever observed. In the course of her career, she'd viewed countless images of the most gruesome offenses. A mutilated toy was nothing in the scheme of things, yet she couldn't help feeling that something truly malevolent had invaded Whispering Springs. She knew that creeping sensation only too well. She'd experienced it at the county jail and inside the courtroom, and she felt it now. A kind of foreboding that slid over her like an oily residue.

Get a grip, she told herself sternly. *It's just a doll*.

But this new discovery changed everything. Jane's effigy couldn't be passed off as business intimidation. For whatever reason, their group was being maliciously targeted.

Ava ran a hand up and down her chilled arm as she stared at the doll, wondering if the threat came from within or from someone on the outside. Someone trapped here with them by the floodwaters, as Dylan had feared. An image came to her of the outbuildings, the bunkhouse and all those empty cabins down by the creek. The property was huge with lots of places to hole up. Someone could hide for days and not be discovered.

She caught Dylan's eye, and he nodded slightly as if he were thinking the same thing. Then his gaze deepened, warning her not to say too much.

The others had come into the room behind them and Ava turned to search each face, taking in Jane's fiery outrage, Celeste's icy aplomb and Blair's twitchy disquiet. Those three women had once been her closest friends, but they were strangers to her now. Any one of them could have left that doll on Jane's bed or started the rock slide that had trapped Ava at the bottom of the canyon in a flash flood. Why someone would do such a thing, she didn't yet know, but she understood better than most that motive was sometimes discernible only to the perpetrator.

She let her gaze linger on all those faces, searching for a guilty sign or tell and wondering if they were doing the same to her.

Blair's hand was at her throat as she gaped wide-eyed at the doll. She started to say something and then seemed to think better of it as she shrank back against the wall. Jane moved to the foot of the bed and Celeste sat down in the nearest chair.

Ava remained at Dylan's side, glad for his stoic presence. She tore her gaze from all those faces and concentrated instead on her surroundings, trying to summon the same objectivity she would use at a crime scene. She noted the time on the bedside clock, the placement of the furniture, the laptop on the desk. Then her gaze moved to the wet boots that had been discarded in a corner of the room.

She came back to Jane. "You said you left your door unlocked when you left, right? Tell me what happened when you got back to the room. Walk me through the chain of events."

Jane shrugged. "Not much to tell. I was soaked so I went straight to the bathroom, stripped and took a quick shower. I didn't see the doll until I came in here to dress."

"That's when you screamed?"

"I saw it first in the mirror. It was so unexpected. I reacted instinctively."

"Understandable," Ava said with a sympathetic nod. "You said you went out for a breath of air. How long were you gone?"

Jane's head came up in defiance. "Why all these questions? Why are you treating *me* like a suspect? I'm the victim here."

"I'm only trying to gather information, Jane."

She took a moment as if deciding whether or not to answer. Then she shrugged. "I don't know how long I was gone. I walked down to the creek to look at the water. I lost track of time."

"You went down there in all this rain? After what happened to me this morning?" Ava's tone turned incredulous. "Why would you do that?"

Jane grew defensive again. "Just because you're careless doesn't mean we all are. I couldn't stay cooped up inside any longer. I was climbing the walls."

"Regardless of how careful you are, you shouldn't go out alone in this weather," Dylan cautioned her. "Especially at night with the water still rising."

Jane glowered at him. "I'm claustrophobic. I had to get out."

"I don't remember you being claustrophobic," Celeste said.

"That's because you don't know anything about me," Jane countered.

"And yet you profess to know me so well."

"You aren't hard to figure out."

Ava put up a hand. "Stop, you two. Please. This isn't helping."

Blair said in a shaky voice, "I don't understand. Dylan, you said the doll was just a way for Tony's rivals to get to him through me."

"What? When did he say that?" Celeste cut in.

Dylan ignored her for the moment. "I said that was a possibility. It seemed a logical conclusion at the time."

Blair gave him a reproachful glance. "But I was right, wasn't I? It's not about the merger. It's about us."

"Wait a minute." Celeste rose from her chair and came over to the bed. "What are you talking about? And what does Tony have to do with any of this? Why did he leave so suddenly? Tell us what's going on, Blair. We have a right to know."

Blair's gaze flicked back to Dylan. "She's

right. We can't keep this from them. Everyone needs to know to take precautions—"

"Precautions? What the *hell* is going on?" Celeste demanded.

"Calm down," Dylan said. "There's no need for anyone to panic."

"How can I calm down with that thing watching me?" Celeste glanced away from the doll. "Can someone throw a blanket over that hideous face?"

"No, don't touch it," Ava said. "We need to bag it and put it with the other one. The cops may be able to retrieve prints."

Celeste's gaze widened. "The *other* one?"

"I found one in my room, too," Blair explained.

"*When?* Why didn't you say anything?"

Jane had been silent for several minutes, but now she came forward, her gaze fixed on Ava. "Why would you think this a police matter? It's just a cruel joke, isn't it? Nothing was taken. No real crime has been committed."

"That's not exactly true." Ava cut her gaze to Blair. "Things have happened that you don't know about."

"Obviously," Celeste muttered.

Blair drew a breath. "A couple of weeks ago, Tony started receiving threatening phone calls at work. A few days later our house was broken into and someone left a message on the bathroom mirror. We thought the incidents were related to a business deal he's involved in, but then last night I found a doll in my room."

Celeste sat down heavily on the edge of the bed as if her knees had suddenly buckled. "Someone is threatening Tony?"

"That's what we thought at first. But now..." Blair trailed away on a helpless shrug.

Jane's gaze dropped from Blair to the doll. Her eyes narrowed and she grew pensive. "What did the one in your room look like?"

"She was porcelain, I think. Like one of those collector's dolls you see on home shopping channels. Blue eyes, blond hair. Dylan thinks she was meant to look like me."

"A *porcelain* doll, you say?"

Blair nodded. "The arms and legs were smashed as if she'd been dropped from a very high place, maybe to simulate a climbing accident."

"What about her throat?"

"I…" Blair glanced at Dylan, as if suddenly realizing the significance of Jane's questions.

"Her neck was twisted like this one," he said.

"But not cut?"

"No."

Celeste swore. "I take it you both knew about this?" She wagged her finger between Dylan and Ava. "And neither of you saw fit to tell us?"

"Don't blame them," Blair said. "I begged them to stay silent. I didn't want to spoil the reunion."

"The *reunion*?" Celeste glared at her in disbelief. "You had no right keeping any of this from us!"

Blair spread her hands in supplication. "I know. That's why I'm telling you now."

"That's not good enough. You should have told us about the threatening phone calls and the break-in before you dragged us all to Whispering Springs. Now we're stranded in this godforsaken place with some psycho leaving murdered dolls in our beds."

"Wow," Jane said. "Impressive. All that righteous indignation. You almost sounded convincing, Celeste."

She whirled. "You can't seriously think I did this."

Jane gave a brittle laugh. "Oh, come on. Blair gets a collector's item and I get a cheap plastic toy. You've never been known for your subtlety, but this is blatant even for you. But I suppose I can understand your lack of imagination. Why put any effort into trolling when you've already threatened me in front of a witness?"

"What the hell are you talking about?"

"Ask Ava. She was right there on the patio with us. She heard you, too."

Ava winced. The last thing she wanted was to be dragged into their bickering, but the accusations had gone on long enough. It was time to defuse the situation before tempers got out of hand. "I don't think she meant it as a threat, Jane. She was just reminding you of what can happen to a climber who gets too cocky."

"She may not have meant it as a threat, but you can't deny she was taunting me. She wanted to get inside my head before the climb today. She knew it was the only way she could beat me to the top of Bishop's Rock."

"This is beyond juvenile and pathetic,

Janie. *Even for you*," Celeste mocked. "And for the record, I could beat you to the top of Bishop's Rock with my eyes closed. I've forgotten more about rock climbing than you will ever know."

"We'll see about that when the weather clears."

"We will, indeed." Celeste paused. "Let me ask you something. If you're so convinced I put that doll in your bed to mess with your head, then how do you explain the one in Blair's room? What possible motive could I have for messing with her head?"

Jane smirked. "You really want to get into that here?"

Something dangerous flashed in Celeste's eyes before she got up and headed for the door. "Whatever. You're clearly mental."

"*I'm* mental? I'm not the one who's spent time in a psychiatric ward."

Celeste stopped and turned back slowly. "What did you say to me?"

Jane's chin came up in defiance. "You heard me. I know all about your time at Cross Creek. And I know about those little pills you used to take. Lily told me *everything*."

Celeste's expression hardened into an icy

mask. "She would never tell you something so personal about me. It's more likely you went snooping through my things."

"Oh, she told me all right. You know why? Because she was afraid of you."

"Don't be ridiculous."

"It's true. Didn't you ever notice how she avoided you? She always had to study when you wanted to come over or she had other plans when you asked her to go shopping. She used every excuse she could come up with to avoid being alone with you."

A shadow of bewilderment crossed Celeste's features. For a moment, it seemed that she might be the one to back down, but then she physically braced herself, straightening her shoulders and steeling her gaze. "I was dealing with depression, you twit. Brought on by the digoxin I was given for a congenital heart defect. It took a while for the doctors to adjust my medication. Lily wasn't afraid of me. She was the only one of you who tried to help me."

Ava stood in mute fascination, her gaze moving from Jane to Celeste, and then, inexplicably, she turned to search for Blair. She had retreated to a safe corner and stood apart from the group as if she wanted to distance herself from all the unpleasantness. Her arms were folded and her head slightly bowed, but she was looking up through her lashes at Celeste. The expression on her face, a certain glint in her eyes, jolted Ava. *She's enjoying this.*

Ava glanced at Dylan, trying to summon his attention, but he was staring across the room at the balcony doors, his focus so intent she felt a prickle of unease at her nape. She followed his gaze, almost afraid that someone stood outside peering in at them.

"What are you looking at?" she asked softly.

He cocked his head. "See those smudges on the door? They're not random smears. Not all of them, anyway. If you look closely, you can make out lettering."

"What?" Ava searched the glass.

"It's written on the outside so you have to read it backward. It's a message."

With the humidity so high from all the rain and the air conditioner running inside, the balcony doors had begun to fog, making the streaks stand out against the night. Still, it took Ava a moment to connect the letters into words. Then her heart thudded in agitation as the impact of the message hit her.

Play the game.

Chapter Nine

"'Play the game.'" Jane read the message aloud as everyone stared in horror at the glass. Her voice held a little catch at the end as if her emotions had gotten the better of her. Someone else said something under her breath and then the room fell eerily silent.

The discovery of the doll had fueled suspicions and accusations within the group, but the message had a unifying effect. Whether they realized it or not, the women had moved closer together, instinctively huddling in the face of an outside threat.

Dylan opened the door, his gaze sweeping across the balcony and the grounds below before he turned back to the glass. The letters had been scrawled with something clear and waxy. He sampled the texture between his fingers and sniffed. When he went back inside, he positioned himself in front the door so that he could protect the evidence while simultaneously keeping an eye on the room. Jane traded places with him, allying herself with the others. They stood on one side of the room, he on the other. Then Ava subtly stepped away and moved around the bed to join him.

She gave him a look and he shook his head, warning her to stay silent. She pulled her cardigan around her as she scanned the room. Dylan could tell she was shaken, but her gaze was steely and determined, giving him a preview of what she would be like in the courtroom. Her age and good looks might initially work against her, but not for long. She would hang back, watching and waiting and allowing her opponent to underestimate her until it was time to move in for the kill.

She cut her eyes back to the trio on the other side of the room as if willing him to search their faces. He followed her lead.

Three pairs of eyes stared back at them.

Then Jane broke the silence, breathlessly repeating the message. "'Play the game.'"

"We heard you the first time," Celeste

snapped. "Besides which, we can read for ourselves." She sat back down, clasping her hands in her lap as if to keep them from trembling.

Blair cleared her throat. "Are they talking about *our* game?"

"What else could it mean? But there is no *they*." Celeste glanced at Jane. "Someone in this room wrote that message. Had to be. How could anyone else know?"

The temporary truce dissolved and Jane turned with an icy stare. "If you're insinuating I wrote that message and planted the doll in my own bed, then you're even crazier than I thought. And believe me, that's saying something."

"You're also wrong that no one else knew," Ava said. "Don't you remember? We occasionally invited some of the girls in Blair's apartment building to join us."

Celeste waved her arm about the room. "Do you see any of them here now?"

"What about you, Dylan?" Jane eyed him suspiciously. "You must have known about the game. Surely Lily mentioned it. Or Ava, perhaps." Her sly gaze lingered.

"This is the first I'm hearing of it," he said.

"And Tony?" Jane turned to Blair. "Does he know?"

Celeste threw up her hands in frustration. "Who cares? In case you haven't noticed, he's not here, either!"

"Why don't you let Blair answer for herself?"

Blair shrugged. "I'm sure I mentioned it at some point. I don't keep secrets from my husband."

"Everyone keeps secrets," Celeste muttered.

"You would know that better than most," Jane observed.

"Ladies," Ava said. "We're all upset and we all want answers, but this incessant squabbling is counterproductive. And it's making my head hurt." She massaged her temples with her fingertips.

"You okay?" Dylan asked at her side.

"I'm fine. Just a little on edge, is all." They both turned their backs to the room as Ava opened the door for a closer look at the message.

"Cherry lip balm," Dylan said.

Ava lifted a brow. "I suppose that's somewhat consistent with the lipstick message left on Blair's mirror." She studied the letters. "Why write it on the outside, I wonder."

"Maybe the perpetrator exited by way of the balcony."

"And the message was a last-minute decision? I somehow doubt that. This is all thought-out. We just haven't yet figured out motive or meaning. It's like our perpetrator was deliberately trying to obscure the letters, but why? If the glass hadn't fogged, the message might have gone undetected in the dark. So why not use red lipstick instead of clear lip balm to get the point across? Why leave a message at all if it's not meant to be found?"

"Why do any of this?" Dylan glanced over his shoulder. "I doubt whoever wrote this would be careless enough to leave a tube of lip balm behind, but I'd still like to have a look around. See if you can get everyone downstairs."

Ava frowned. "How do you propose I do that?"

"You'll think of something."

"What are you two whispering about?" Celeste demanded.

"Nothing. Just pondering our next move." Ava shot Dylan a sidelong look before she turned back to the group. She was all business now, shoulders rigid, jaw set in determination, and yet something in that glance—the hooded eyes, the way she looked up through her lashes—reminded him a little too vividly of what they'd been doing only half an hour ago.

He fought those images, turning back to the window as he monitored the conversation behind him.

"And just what is our next move?" Celeste asked.

Ava lifted her hair off her neck and wound it in a coil at the back of her head. "We've done all we can up here. It's been a long day. Why don't we go downstairs, have a drink and regroup? Maybe we could all pitch in and make dinner. That'll give us something productive to focus on. Being at each other's throats is only making the situation more stressful."

Celeste got to her feet. "I don't cook, but I could certainly go for a drink."

Jane planted herself beside the bed with an obstinate scowl. "Wait. Everyone wait just a damn minute. Aren't we going to talk about this?"

"What do you think we've been doing?" Celeste headed for the door.

"We can hash it out downstairs in a calm, civilized manner," Ava said. "Dylan can deal with everything up here."

That suggestion drew a deeper scowl. "What does that mean?"

"I'll take care of the doll and the window," he said. "Just go downstairs and relax."

Jane folded her arms. "Sounds like you're trying to get rid of us. Or worse, you want to sweep everything under the rug the way we did with Lily's suicide."

The accusation drew a strained hush, maybe because Jane's accusation hit a little too close to home. Dylan had refused to wear the same hair shirt that Ava had donned after Lily's death, but he'd had his moments of guilt. There had been nights when he'd lain awake wondering what he might have done differently. Maybe if he'd found a gentler way of ending things…if he'd pressed harder for answers when she called so upset…if he'd given her a shoulder to lean on…a sympathetic ear…

Water under the bridge, he told himself grimly. Lily was dead and life had moved on. For most of them, anyway.

He turned once more to search their faces.

Maybe it was his imagination, but they all looked guilty of something. Even Ava. She averted her eyes as she tugged down her sweater sleeve.

Jane said into that electrified silence, "Hit a nerve, didn't I? Good. I want you to be uncomfortable. I want to make you all think. I'm not leaving this room until I say what's on my mind."

Ava sighed. "Then say it."

Jane moved her gaze slowly around the space, lingering on each of them. "We only ever talked about Lily's suicide in the most superficial terms. We never dug deep. We never shared our honest feelings or admitted our guilt. And we were guilty. Every single one of us. We knew she was in trouble and we did nothing to help her."

"Speak for yourself," Celeste muttered.

Jane ignored her. "What was she even doing on that rooftop to begin with? Have any of you ever asked yourself that question?"

"That you have to ask reveals how little you knew about her," Celeste said. "She used to go up there all the time. She liked looking at the lights."

"That doesn't explain why she jumped."

"There were no satisfactory answers ten years ago and there won't be now," Ava said, refusing to meet Dylan's gaze.

"You don't know that," Jane insisted. "That's why we need to play the game. It's the only way we can get everything out into the open."

"Have you forgotten what happened the last time we played?" Ava asked.

Dylan glanced at her. "What did happen?"

"Long story," she murmured. "Maybe now isn't the best time to get into it."

"Now is the perfect time." Jane turned to Dylan. "It was the night before Lily died. Things were said that couldn't be unsaid."

"Such as?"

"First, we should give you a little background." Jane sat down on the edge of the bed, relishing her time in the spotlight. "We called it the Game of Secrets. The object was to reveal something about oneself or about someone else that the rest of us didn't know. We took great pains to keep everything anonymous. We disguised our handwriting by printing our secrets on identical pieces of paper. Then we folded the notes just so and placed them in a bowl. This would go on throughout the evening. After a few hours, the bowl would be nearly full. That's when the real game started."

"Which was?"

"Drawing out our indiscretions one by one and reading them aloud."

"Sounds like a good way to create hard feelings," Dylan said.

"Most of the time it was fairly innocuous stuff," Ava explained. She looked uneasy. "Cheating on an exam, flirting with someone's boyfriend, that sort of thing. High school stuff, really. Behavior we should have outgrown before college. But it was sometimes cathartic. Like a confessional. An anonymous way of getting things off your chest."

"But it escalated," he said.

"We started upping the ante. Drinking more, revealing more..." She hesitated. "You get the picture. Things would sometimes get out of hand and people would end up hurt."

"What happened the last time you played?"

She fiddled with a button on her sweater. "I really don't see the point of getting into this right now. We're all tense. Let's just take a break. All of us," she said to the room.

Jane's chin came back up. "I'm not leaving until you agree to play."

"Jane, for God's sake—"

"Come on, Ava. The others will do it if you agree. Even Celeste. Just one last time. If not for me, then for Lily. We may never see each other again and there are things that still need to be said."

Ava stopped fidgeting and looked Jane square in the eyes with cold deliberation. "No. I don't want any part of this. I think it's a terrible idea. The last thing we need is more bickering. If you all want to play, then go ahead, but count me out."

Celeste seemed all too happy to egg her on. "You tell her, Ava. I'm with you."

"Well, I'm not." Blair's declaration was so unexpected, everyone turned to her in shock. She shrugged to soften the blow. "Sorry, Ava, but I'm on Jane's side this time. I think we should play. It's for the best."

Ava stared at her in disbelief. "Best for who?"

"All of us. Jane's right. There are still things that need to be said. Questions that need to be answered." Even as she addressed Ava, she focused in on Celeste. "Secrets that need to be shared."

"You're asking for trouble," Ava warned.

Blair smiled. "When did that ever stop us?"

DYLAN WATCHED IN RELIEF as the group filed into the hallway. It had taken a fair amount of coercion and persuasion, but Ava had finally managed to herd them out the door. Jane had argued until the bitter end, managing to wear Ava down until she'd agreed to at least think about participating in the game. But Ava hadn't been happy about it. The look she'd flashed Dylan over her shoulder warned him to make short work of his search. She had no intention of assuming the role of referee for the rest of the evening.

He took out his phone and snapped a few shots of the doll and then the message from both sides of the glass. He conducted a careful search of the bedroom and bathroom, checking drawers and Jane's toiletries, but no tube of lip balm turned up. Using the plastic bag from the trash can, he collected the doll and took it to his room for closer scrutiny later. When he opened the door to return to Jane's room, Ava stood in the hallway.

"I thought you'd gone downstairs." He took a quick glance down the corridor before motioning her inside.

She looked nervous as she entered the room. "I did, but I told them I wanted to shower and change before we start dinner. The others may want to do the same, so if you haven't finished in Jane's room, you'll need to make quick work of it."

"No worries. I'm done."

"Did you find anything?"

"Nothing incriminating."

"What did you do with the doll?"

"I put it with the other one. Until we know what we're dealing with, we should try to preserve as much evidence as we can. We don't know how long we'll be stuck here." *Or what else might happen.*

"Dylan, what *are* we dealing with?" She stood with her back to the window. "This is all so bizarre. First Blair finds a look-alike doll in her bed and now Jane? Who's next? Me? Celeste? You? This can't be about Tony's business. He's not even here and things just keep getting stranger and stranger."

She looked so unsettled, Dylan had to resist the urge to pull her into his arms, but he didn't think his protective instincts would be particularly welcome at that moment. Bad things were happening and they both needed to keep a clear head. "Maybe Tony's absence is by design rather than accident."

"You think he has something to do with all this? Even the phone calls and break-in?"

"I'm not ruling anyone out at this point."

Ava rubbed her temples with her fingertips. "God, this headache."

"Have you taken anything for it?"

"It's just tension. I've learned to live with it."

"Here, let me try something." He stepped behind her, rotating his thumbs counterclockwise on her temples and then finding the pressure points at the base of her skull. After a moment, she let her head fall back against him. "Better?"

"Yes, thank you. Magic hands." She reached up and laced her fingers through his, drawing his arms over her shoulders and around her. The ease and comfort of the action surprised Dylan. It was like they had been together for years, but he didn't know if that was a good thing or not. He held her for a moment before releasing her.

She folded her arms and picked up their conservation as if there'd been no interlude. "You know how I feel about Tony Redding. I've never trusted him, and after what you told me about his assignation with Celeste last night, I could easily believe he's up to something. But these dolls don't seem his style."

"Maybe that's the point," Dylan said.

"You think he's using them as misdirection? That's possible, I guess. He's not a stupid man. To the contrary, he's always struck me as clever and cunning. Maybe he and Celeste have cooked up something together. Notice she and I are the only ones who haven't gotten a doll."

"Yet," Dylan said.

"Yet," she agreed.

"What exactly do you mean by 'cooked up'? What kind of scheme are you suggesting?"

Ava lowered her voice. "Celeste reminded me last night that Blair is the one with the real money in that relationship. If Tony were to divorce her, he might be left out in the cold. He wouldn't be the first husband to come up with an alternate plan."

"Let's not get ahead of ourselves. It's a big leap from mutilated dolls to homicide."

She shrugged. "Not that big. You'd be surprised at the number of spousal murder cases that come across my desk in any given year. Some of the schemes are so flaky you'd think a two-year-old came up with them. As in all things, it's smart to follow the money. Greed as motive is right up there with sex and revenge."

"Where does Jane figure into this scheme?"

"She doesn't. I have a whole different theory about her. But if we're talking misdirection, placing a doll in her own bed and leaving a message on the bedroom window would be classic."

"To what end?" Dylan studied Ava's features as she pondered the problem. It was fascinating to follow her thought processes.

"To manipulate us into playing the game, of course. She obviously has something she wants to reveal, about herself or someone else, and she craves an audience. You saw how relentless she was. One might even say obsessed." Ava fell silent, deep in contemplation. "I have to say, this reunion has been a real eye-opener. I'm not only talking about the dolls or the messages or what happened to me in the canyon. I'm talking about *them*. The people who used to be my closest friends. Maybe I'm being too harsh, but I can't help wondering what I ever saw in any of them. Jane said the same thing last night. She said I wasn't like the others, but I'm not so sure about that. For whatever reason, I once gravitated to their pettiness and duplicity. Their mean-spirited games. No one twisted my arm. They're not likable people, Dylan. Maybe I'm not, either."

"There's a reason you haven't kept in touch," he said. "You grew up. You moved on. They didn't."

"I like to think that I've matured, but then I go and do something stupid like lose my temper in court." She winced. "But you're right about the others. The dynamics haven't changed. Celeste and Jane have already declared war and the rivalry between Celeste and Blair will get ugly if we play the game. For them, it's not about clearing the air. It's a psychological ambush."

"Then play it," Dylan said. "Let them tip their hands."

"No matter how vicious it gets?"

"It may be the best chance we have of getting to the bottom of things before someone gets hurt."

"I guess." But she didn't sound convinced.

"Ava?"

She closed her eyes briefly as if anticipating his next question.

"What happened the last time you played? You said things got out of hand?"

She sighed. "It's not something I like to talk about. My behavior still bothers me after all these years."

"What did you do?"

She turned to him reluctantly. "Lily and I had a terrible fight that night."

"What about?"

"You."

He said in surprise, "She knew about us? You never told me."

"I wanted to, but I was too ashamed. It was such an unpleasant confrontation. Some of the things she said struck a nerve. Other things…" Ava paused on a shiver. "She wasn't herself that night. At times she seemed borderline incoherent. I thought she'd had too much to drink, but now I know that she'd gone to a very dark place. The attack on me was so uncharacteristic. I think it was her way of letting me know she was in trouble. But I didn't see it. Maybe I didn't want to."

"Did the others witness the argument?"

"I don't think so, but a lot of other stuff

went down that night. We'd all taken a break and Lily and I had gone out to the balcony for some air. She leaned over the railing, too far for my comfort, and when I grabbed her arm to pull her back, she turned on me. It was like an explosion. I was caught off guard and my instinct was to fight back. We both said a lot of terrible things to each other and that was our last conversation. The last time I ever saw her."

Dylan took her hand and she glanced up. Her impulse was to pull away. He could see the resistance in her eyes. But she held her ground even when he slid his fingers up to her shoulder. "I'm beginning to understand something now. You didn't just feel guilty about us. You blamed yourself for Lily's death."

"Rationally I knew I wasn't responsible, but emotionally…" She paused on a shaky breath. "You've no idea how many times I've relived that argument in my head."

He put both hands on her shoulders. "You said things in the heat of the moment. You're human. You weren't to blame for Lily's suicide. Something had gone very wrong in her world and none of us saw it. I've said it a thousand times and I'll say it again. We didn't do anything wrong."

"But what if someone thinks we did?"

Chapter Ten

"You mean Jane."

Ava nodded. "I keep going back to what you once said about her devotion to Lily."

"That doesn't make her guilty of anything," Dylan said.

"I know. But you honed in on something back then. You saw something in her behavior that the rest of us didn't." Ava paused. "Or maybe I'm just picking on Jane because I'd rather believe her capable of malicious trickery than contemplate a more dire plot by Tony Redding. And it makes about as much sense as anything else—" She broke off as she glanced toward the hallway door. A sound came to her, too faint to identify, but loud enough to alarm her. "Did you hear that?"

Dylan listened for a moment, then put a

finger to his lips. He crossed the room quietly and Ava followed. She hung back as he opened the door and glanced both ways down the hallway. Then he disappeared outside, only to return a moment later with a shrug. "If someone was here, they must have stepped into another room. These walls are pretty thin. Let's go out on the balcony to finish our discussion."

"I really should get back downstairs before Celeste and Jane kill each other," Ava said. "I only wish I was kidding about that."

Dylan's gaze met hers. His intensity thrilled her. She was amazed how easily he could make her heart jump with nothing more than a look. "Stay a minute. I have something else I want to talk to you about."

He moved around her to open the glass doors and she stepped outside. The balcony was shadowy with only the lamplight spilling from the room to illuminate the dark corners. No one would be able to see them from the ground, and the hard rain would drown out their voices. It was like hiding in a cocoon, Ava thought. Sequestered in a private little world all their own.

Things were moving so quickly she'd had

no chance to process their time together. But now, in the lull, images came floating back to her. A heated whisper. A lingering kiss. The feathery skim of his lips at her throat...

She stood facing the night, but she watched him from the corner of her eye. He was a tall man, lean and tough, and yet there was an unexpected grace in the way he carried himself. Something quietly sensual in the way he tipped his head, enjoying the cool spray from the raindrops hitting the overhang.

Ava wrapped her arms around her middle, tracing his silhouette, remembering the weight of him, the feel of him, the scent of him. But even as her pulse fluttered to life, weariness descended. She felt worn out, not so much from the danger and intrigue, but from the drag of old memories and the burden of too many regrets.

And she did have regrets. She could never admit that before, even to herself, because the consequences of her decision had been too painful. Best to move on, stay focused, live each day as it came. Houston had been good to her. She had a fulfilling career and a loving family nearby. She was as close to content as a neurotic workaholic was ever likely to be, and she knew better than anyone that no good came from dwelling on missed opportunities.

But seeing Dylan again had dredged up a hard truth. Sending him away had been the worst mistake of her life, no matter the justification. They'd had something special, the kind of love that could have grown stronger and deeper through the years, but she'd thrown it all away for reasons that had mostly been trifling. In some ways, that was the most painful part. The hardest truth to accept. Maybe she wouldn't feel such a loss if one of them had committed an egregious betrayal or deception. Maybe she wouldn't look back on the past ten years and think, *My God, what a waste.*

"Ava?"

She sighed inwardly. "Yes?"

He stood looking down at her, head slightly cocked. "Where did you go just now? You got so quiet. Like you were a million miles away."

"Oh, I was just thinking about everything that's happened." She lifted her hands to tuck back her hair, surprised to find that they were trembling.

"Everything?" She couldn't see his expression clearly in the shadows, but she heard a subtle shift in his tone. His voice deepened, roughened. "We didn't have a chance earlier to talk about what happened between us."

She looked over at him with a smile. "What's there to say, really? It happened. It was amazing. End of story, right?"

"I guess it has to be for now. We've a lot on our plates."

Was that regret she heard in his voice? Or was she projecting? "We should probably get back to it, then."

"Ava." A whisper. An entreaty.

She melted.

He tugged her to him, kissing her hair, her forehead and then her lips. She wrapped her arms around him and held on tightly, kissing him back with the kind of fervor she hadn't felt in years.

He pulled away, his eyes glinting in the darkness. "What was that about?"

"Nothing. Everything. Now we can get back to business."

Her voice sounded steady, but inside she reeled. A part of her wanted to cling to him forever even as her brain warned they were moving too fast. This might not be a one-time-only thing. They needed to slow down. Think things through. Be smart. Impetuosity had never served her well.

She turned back to the rain, putting a subtle distance between them even as her fingertips fluttered to her lips. "In all this discussion about motives, we haven't talked about Blair yet."

"What about her?"

"I noticed something earlier. I don't think you could see her from your position, but she had this look in her eyes when Celeste and Jane were fighting and a sort of sly smile that caught me by surprise. Like she was enjoying their dustup. And then she was so quick to take Jane's side. I wonder if she knows about Celeste and Tony and that's why she wants to play the game."

"To goad Celeste into a confession?"

"Or to publicly humiliate her. I can only guess at her reasoning, but her demeanor seemed off. And now that we're talking about Blair, something else has occurred to me. Do you think you can get back into her suite without being seen?"

"Not easily, but it can be done. Why?"

"If the glass hadn't fogged in Jane's room,

we might have missed the message until daylight. What if we overlooked something in Blair's room?"

"Another message, you mean?"

"It's a long shot, but we should check to make certain."

"I'll take a look later tonight if you can keep everyone occupied."

"How will you get in?"

"Let me worry about that. You just make sure no one comes upstairs until you hear from me."

"There's only one way I can make certain of that," she said with a grimace. "I'll have to play their stupid game."

"The game has already started, Ava. Someone has been playing us from the moment we arrived at Whispering Springs."

"I know."

"It's good you suggested we search Blair's suite. We should go through all the rooms. It's not enough that you and I have each other's backs. We need to go on the offensive."

She nodded as she searched the drenched landscape. If possible, the night seemed to grow darker. Ava could barely trace the escarpment against the deeper black of the sky.

The coyotes had gone silent, driven to high ground by the flood. But the evening was far from quiet. Over the steady drumbeat of rain, she could hear the rumble of thunder and the distant roar of rushing water in the creek.

Beside her, Dylan had gone very still, his gaze fixed on the woods. Then his hand went to his back, touching but not drawing his weapon.

"What is it?" she whispered.

"Someone's out there."

DYLAN STARED AT the tree line. He could see nothing now, no distinction between night and shadow, but he'd spotted a flicker of illumination a moment ago and what he thought might be a hunched silhouette watching the house.

"I saw a light," he said. "Just beyond that row of pinions."

Ava's gaze narrowed as she peered into the trees. "Are you sure it wasn't lightning?"

"Too low and close for lightning. *There*. Right there. Did you see it? Someone's in the woods with a flashlight."

"I see it now," she said. "The light is moving away from the house. Who do you suppose is out there? Dylan." She moved closer to him. "Do you think they saw us up here?"

"It's possible we spooked them away. There's a trail just beyond those trees that leads back to the cabins."

"But the cabins are empty," Ava said. "Blair told me so herself. She made sure all the other guests had checked out before we arrived so we could have the place to ourselves." Her gaze narrowed as she peered into the woods. "Why would anyone be out there in this weather?"

"It could be Noah. He told me earlier he's moved into one of the cabins until the water recedes. It's a good place to keep an eye on the creek and a lookout for looters."

"Looters? We're miles from anywhere and the roads are all flooded."

"That's hardly a deterrent. Boats can come in and out. Someone working alone may not be much of a threat, but if they travel in a pack, things could get dicey." Dylan drew his weapon and placed it in her hand. "Take this and go downstairs. Make sure all the windows and doors are locked and keep everyone inside."

She looked at him in alarm. "You're not

going out there, are you? You just said things could get dicey."

"It's my job to go out there. That's why Blair hired me, remember?"

"Well, you can't go unarmed. That's crazy." Ava pushed the gun back into his hand. "You need this more than we do. Could be anyone out there. A looter, a criminal. God knows. We'll be fine here. Safety in numbers, remember?"

He tucked the weapon back in his jeans. "Make sure everyone stays inside until I get back."

"I will. Just please be careful."

He touched her face briefly and then turned, vaulted over the railing and hung for a split second before dropping to the ground with a splash.

DYLAN COULD SMELL the loamy odor of the floodwaters as he made his way along the rugged trail. The darkness of the woods was impenetrable. Without the moon and stars to guide him, he traveled mostly by instinct and memory, glad that he'd taken the extra days to familiarize himself with the terrain. He moved unerringly westward, grounded by the sound of rushing water.

The darkness was so complete he had flashbacks to his time in the desert. The sameness of the topography could be disorienting under the best of conditions, but in a sandstorm with fifty-mile-an-hour swirling winds, it was hard to tell up from down, much less east from west. He'd learned quickly not to panic. It was too easy to lose one's head and wander around for hours. In unfamiliar terrain surrounded by the enemy, best to hunker down and wait it out, but that took a special kind of fortitude.

Those days were long behind him, but his instincts hadn't left him. The back of his neck bristled a warning and he froze in concentration, filtering out the drumming of the rain as he tried to vector in on a new sound. Nothing he could pinpoint, but he worried that someone was coming up behind him. He left the path, taking refuge in the trees until he could determine if the coast was clear.

Rain pounded his face and ran down his collar as he waited. He could see nothing in front or behind him but darkness and rain. He was tempted to take out his cell phone for illumination, but if someone was behind him, he didn't want to give away his position or, worse, damage his only connection to the outside world. The thought occurred to him as he returned to the trail that he might have been lured away from the house on purpose. He trusted Ava to lock up and make sure everyone stayed inside, but without a weapon, they were vulnerable. And what about the danger from within?

A dozen scenarios flashed through his head, none of them good, and he had a moment of uncharacteristic doubt. But second-guessing was the bane of any operation. He'd learned that lesson the hard way. He pressed on, following his instincts and the rumble of the creek.

The roar grew louder as he came out of the woods. He stood at the top of the embankment, gazing down at the raging water, but he knew better than to linger for too long with his back to the trees. Wiping raindrops from his eyes, he traveled along the ridge until he came to the first of the cabins. It was perched on the edge of the bluff with a back deck hanging over the creek. A good place to keep a check on rising water.

Dylan circled around to the front, disappearing into the shadows for a few minutes as he watched the cabin. The windows were dark. He could see no sign of life within or without. He eased closer, moving up the wooden steps with barely a sound. A pair of rain boots had been discarded on the porch floor and a yellow rain slicker hung from a wall peg. He started to call out Noah's name, but then he noticed the front door had been left open a crack.

He drew his weapon and flattened himself against the porch wall as he listened intently. When no sound came to him, he pushed open the door and stepped quickly across the threshold. He didn't turn on the overhead light. Instead, he used the flashlight app on his phone, angling the beam slowly around the room.

The interior of the cabin was similar to the accommodations in the main house—rustic cedar flooring, plush rugs and well-worn leather furniture grouped around a stone fireplace. A bar separated a tiny kitchenette from the living space, and a narrow hallway led back to the bedroom and bathroom. Glass doors opened to the back deck, and he imagined in daylight and better weather, the view would be spectacular.

But it was only a fleeting thought because as he moved the light around the room, strewn papers on the floor in front of the fireplace caught his attention. Then he noticed the open drawers and scattered chair cushions. The tossed books and crooked artwork. The place had been thoroughly ransacked, perhaps by looters looking for cash and small valuables.

Dylan remained at the threshold as he took in the chaos. Then he shone the beam across the room and out the deck doors, tracing the outline of the guardrail and the silhouette of a covered hot tub. If the slicker and boots on the front porch belonged to Noah, where was he?

As silent as a ghost, Dylan crossed the room and stood at the deck doors, listening to the night sounds all around him—the rain, the creek, the rustle of wind in the trees. From somewhere inside the cabin came the sound of dripping water.

He moved down the hallway, toeing open the first door and assuming a defensive position as he swung the light around the room. The bed linens had been yanked from the mattress and a duffel bag of clothing and toiletries had been dumped on the floor. The closet was empty, as were the dresser drawers that had been left open.

Dylan backed out of the room, following the sound of dripping water across the hall to the bathroom. The door was open and he took a quick assessment of the space before turning on the light. A sudden movement spiked his pulse before he realized he'd caught a glimpse of his reflection in the mirror.

He put away his phone and used both hands to steady his weapon as instinct and dread prickled his scalp. The drip of the faucet was like a metronome, measuring his accelerated heartbeat. He could hear the thud of rain on the roof and the roar of the creek twenty feet below the cabin, but the outside noises receded as his senses focused in on the *plop...plop...plop* of water droplets hitting porcelain.

But it wasn't so much the leaky faucet that alarmed him as the smell that accompanied the sound. Beneath the fragrance of pine cleaner was the coppery tang of a butcher shop.

He turned slowly, his gaze moving to the shower curtain. Ironically, pine trees decorated the fabric, matching the scent that clung to his nostrils. In the split second before he lifted his hand to pull back the curtain, he noticed a crimson streak across the wall. He glanced back at the vanity, noting a smear on one of the fixtures and another along the white backsplash. It was as if someone with bloody hands had haphazardly washed up before fleeing the cabin.

He turned back to the shower curtain. *Plop...plop...plop...*

He readied his weapon. *Plop...plop...plop...*

He pulled back the fabric. *Plop...plop... plop...*

The tub was empty and pristine. Nothing to see. No crumpled body. No bloody splashes against the subway tile.

He blew out a breath, releasing the movie image that had played in his head. Then he made another sweep of the bathroom, hallway and bedroom. Returning to the living area, he turned on the overhead light, once again taking note of the disorder. For several long moments he stood there listening to the silence. There were no darting shadows, no creaking floorboards, but he had a strong feeling he wasn't alone. He scanned the glass deck doors and all the windows in the living area, almost expecting to find someone peering in from the darkness. Nothing.

This wasn't like him, being so on edge. He was reminded of the early days of his first deployment when even the slightest sound or movement had been like a buzz saw across his nerve endings. He mentally shook himself and went outside to the deck.

Turning on the flashlight app, he aimed the beam all over the floorboards and along the railing. The rain was still coming down hard, a steady, dismal pound that wore on his ragged nerves. He leaned over the railing, tracing wooden steps to the creek and catching glimpses of frothing water through pine boughs. All the while, he couldn't shake the notion that someone was out there in the darkness, watching his every move.

He turned, keeping the trees in his peripheral vision as he once again searched the deck. He played the light around the corners and even up to the roof. Then his gaze came back to the hot tub. A blue plastic cover had been thrown over the top to keep leaves and debris from the water. He placed his phone on the deck and tugged off the tarp. The darkness was so complete he didn't see anything at first. He reached for his phone, slanting the beam down into the water.

Glassy eyes stared back at him.

Not doll eyes this time, but the frosted gaze of a dead man.

Chapter Eleven

Dylan had seen dead bodies before and enough blood and gore to fuel a lifetime of nightmares, but somehow those sightless eyes staring up at him through water still had the power to shock him.

Noah Pickett lay on the bottom of the tub, face turned skyward as if waiting for someone to come and peel back the cover of his prison. Dylan knew the man was dead, but he still felt compelled to check for a pulse. He reached down into the water and drew him up, holding the body with one arm while he checked for a pulse in the throat and then at the wrist.

The skin was cold, the joints stiff. Dylan guessed he had been dead for several hours, bludgeoned at the temple, the face and the base of his skull. He may have had other injuries that were not apparent in the dark. Dylan was no forensics expert, but it seemed likely that Noah had been caught by surprise on the deck. The blow to the base of the skull had taken him down and the other strikes were either rage or insurance. If the vicious attack hadn't killed him, he would have drowned.

Dylan let the body slip back down into the tub and then he stepped away, flinging water from his hands as icy fear gripped him. Not for himself, but for Ava and the others back at the ranch house. Mutilated dolls were one thing, but murder took everything to a whole different level.

He reached for his phone and his weapon, turning once more to face the night. He didn't want to be caught unaware like poor Noah. He scanned the trees and all along the steps. *Where are you?* Who *are you?*

The no-service screen sent another chill through him. Either the storm had taken out the nearest tower or the signal was deliberately blocked. Either way, Dylan needed to get back to the main house to use the landline.

He placed the tarp back over the hot tub and glanced around. He'd already contaminated the crime scene, but no help for that now. Self-preservation had already kicked in and he rose quickly, checking his surroundings once more before going back inside. The chaotic search of the house took on a new connotation. It wasn't the careless hunt of a looter, he now knew. In all likelihood, Noah's killer had been looking for something specific.

Dylan went back down the hall to the bedroom, sifting through the rumpled bed linens and clothing before crossing the hall to the bathroom. He used the tail of his shirt to open vanity drawers, cabinets and the toilet lid. All the while, he told himself he was wasting valuable time. He needed to be on his way to the ranch. He needed that landline.

He was just headed out the front door when a gust of wind rippled through the papers on the floor. He shut the door, turned on the overhead light and retraced his steps across the room. Hunkering in front of the fireplace, he used his gun to sort through a dozen or more newspaper clippings, noting dates and headlines before he took the time to scan the articles about a young woman named Sara Rainey. An employee of the ranch, she'd disappeared from Whispering Springs seven years ago. The articles chronicled the subsequent search and police investigation, which had gone on for weeks, but no trace of the woman had ever been found.

A few photographs were mixed in with the clippings, one a shot of a teenage couple at the top of Bishop's Rock. Even years younger and with a different hairstyle, Noah Pickett was instantly recognizable. His companion was the girl from the newspaper articles. The pair beamed for the camera, two young lovers on a climb with no thought to the violent future that awaited them.

The other photographs had been taken at various locations around Whispering Springs, including the canyon where Ava had been trapped. Spreading everything out on the floor, Dylan snapped a few shots with his phone and then rose.

He had no idea what he'd stumbled onto, what any of this had to do with the reunion, the dolls or Tony Redding's business. But he'd been right earlier about the game. It had begun long before he and Ava had arrived at Whispering Springs.

And the stakes couldn't be higher.

"Earth to Ava."

Blair waved a hand in front of her face and she started. "I'm sorry. What?"

Blair smiled. "Finally got your attention. I called to you when I came down the stairs. I thought you were ignoring me." She looked very pretty in a blue V-neck sweater that set off her eyes. Unfortunately, when Ava looked at her, all she could see was the mangled doll on Blair's bed.

"I didn't hear you." Ava glanced around. "Where are the others?"

"I don't know. Upstairs probably. What were you looking at so intently just now?"

"I was watching the rain."

Blair cocked her head, giving her a sidelong scrutiny. "I thought perhaps you were looking for Dylan. I saw him head out toward the woods a little while ago. He seemed in a hurry. Any idea where he was going?"

Ava tucked back her hair. "I imagine he was doing a perimeter check. You did hire him to keep an eye on the place, right?"

"Yes, for all the good it's done."

Ava's hackles rose in spite of herself. "That's hardly fair. Whispering Springs is a big property with lots of rugged terrain and plenty of places to hide. He can't be everywhere at once."

"Oh, I know. I didn't mean to sound as if I were chastising him. He recommended that I beef up security. It was my decision not to."

"Because you didn't want Tony to catch on."

"I explained all that yesterday. And despite the way I sounded just now, I do trust Dylan. I can't think of anyone I'd rather have watching out for us. I'm just on edge."

"We all are," Ava said. "But we have to stay calm and on guard. We'll be okay."

"I can't believe all this is happening," Blair lamented. "The violation of our home was bad enough, but those dolls are just plain sinister. I can't believe I'm saying this, but I hope someone *is* playing a cruel joke on us. But something keeps going through my mind. The broken limbs, the slashed throat. Ava…what if someone is warning us of their intent?"

That thought had crossed Ava's mind, as well, but she thought it best to keep her worries to herself. Blair was jittery enough. "Don't let your imagination get the better of you. Like I said, we need to remain calm. No going off without telling anyone. No hiking or climbing or roaming the grounds alone. Windows and doors remain locked, even in the daytime. Basically, use common sense. We need to stick together until we can get out of this place. It would also help if we stop fighting among ourselves."

"That may be easier said than done. Celeste is out for blood. Jane isn't much better." Absently Blair drew a heart on the window with her fingertip. "Haven't you wondered why you and Celeste are the only ones who haven't gotten dolls?"

"I've only been here two days. Maybe whoever is responsible just hasn't gotten around to me yet. There's still time. We may be stuck here until the end of the week."

Blair traced a heart within a heart. "What if someone is out there right now watching us? We can't see them, but they can see us."

"Blair, stop."

She squeezed one eye closed, her finger paused in the center of the smallest heart as if taking aim. "I can sense a presence out there. Can't you?"

"No one's out there."

"But what if they are? What if someone followed us here?"

"What are you talking about, Blair? Have you seen someone suspicious hanging around the ranch?"

"No, but it could be anyone. A disgruntled former employee. An old lover. Maybe someone we crossed in college. Have you thought about that? We weren't the nicest people back then. We were all so smug in our own little bubble. No thought to anyone else. So above it all. No time even to take care of our own friend."

"You mean Lily."

Blair shot her a glance. "Jane has a point, you know. We never really talked about what happened."

Ava frowned. "Is that why you want to play the game?"

"The game is just a distraction."

"From what?"

"From the weather. From each other. From whoever is out there." Blair turned back to the window. "Sometimes I worry that our past will catch up with us. We may have enemies we don't even know about."

The strange conversation unsettled Ava.

"Because we were a little too full of ourselves? Come on, Blair. You're getting a little carried away with all this."

"I didn't imagine those dolls, did I? Or the message on Jane's window?" She dropped her finger from the glass, revealing a hole in the center of the heart. "Someone is after us. I'm just trying to figure out who it could be."

Ava said reluctantly, "It would have to be someone with access to room keys."

"Or someone who knows how to pick locks. It's not that hard. I taught myself years ago watching YouTube videos. I got tired of locking myself out all the time." Blair glanced over her shoulder before bringing her lips close to Ava's ear. "Do you trust the others?"

Ava froze as Blair's warm breath feathered against her cheek. For a moment she could have sworn she smelled cherry lip balm. She pulled away, trying to hide her trepidation, but her heart was suddenly pounding so hard she could scarcely draw a breath. She resisted the temptation to take a step back as she said carefully, "I don't know. I haven't been around either of them in years. Do you trust them?"

"Celeste, never. She's always been a backstabber." Blair turned away, refocusing her attention on the glass. She drew one heart after another until half a dozen were nested inside one another.

There's meaning in that drawing, Ava thought. She just didn't yet know what to make of it. "What about Jane?"

"Jane has a malicious streak, but I don't think she's really dangerous."

"And you think Celeste is?"

"She would do anything to get what she wants. But I can hardly fault her for that." Blair obliterated the hearts with a single swipe of her hand. "So would I if it came down to it."

Ava tried to keep her tone even. "What do you think she wants?"

"Wow, that lightning is getting close," Blair murmured.

"Answer my question," Ava demanded.

"Forget Celeste. We've bigger things to worry about."

Ava searched Blair's profile. "Like what?"

She shrugged. "The weather, of course. Another storm is moving in. You know what that means, don't you? Things will get worse before they get better."

"That's an ominous way of putting it."
Ava peered through the darkness toward the
woods. She wished Dylan would come back.
He'd been gone for a long time and she was
starting to get anxious. She kept reminding
herself that he was a highly trained former
army ranger who could handle himself in any
situation. He would be fine. Safer out there,
perhaps, than she was in here with Blair and
the others. Still, Ava couldn't stifle a niggling
worry that something was wrong.

She watched Blair's reflection in the window. She held her hands in front of her,
unconsciously twisting her diamond engage-
ment ring as she monitored the lightning.

"Blair? Are you sure you're okay?"

She glanced at Ava. "Yes. Why?"

"The way you keep twisting that engage-
ment ring. It's almost as if you want to rip
off your finger."

Blair dropped her hands to her sides. "It's a
habit. I fidget when I'm anxious. I'll feel better when Dylan gets back. I don't mean to be
one of those women who always needs a man
for protection, but..." She glanced toward the
entrance hall. "What if someone tries to get
in the house while he's gone?"

"Don't borrow trouble."

"I know, I know. Don't mind me. The weather is making me like this. We're all a little stir-crazy, I think. Where did you say Dylan went?"

"He's making rounds. He'll be back soon enough. Just try to relax, okay? Maybe we should go out to the kitchen and start dinner. Get our minds on something else."

"I'm not hungry." Lightning cracked and the lights flickered. Blair caught her breath. "Oh, no."

"Don't worry. If the power goes out, the generator will kick in. We'll be fine," Ava said. "But let's move away from the windows. You're right. That lightning is getting closer. And we should locate some candles just to be on the safe side."

"You're giving me busywork," Blair accused.

"Is it working?"

"I'll light some candles and let you know." She took a long match from a box on the hearth and lit the pillar candles on the mantel. Ava watched her move about the room, lighting votives in glass holders. Then she took a crystal bowl from a locked cabinet and placed it on the coffee table. Dimming the lights, she stood back to admire her handiwork.

"What's the bowl for?" Ava asked.

Blair cut her a glance. "Do you have to ask? It's for the secrets."

"Nice ambience," a voice said from the archway. "Almost makes you forget that we're stuck here."

"Celeste?" Blair peered across the room.

She sauntered into the great room and plopped down in a leather armchair, throwing her legs over the side. "Who else would it be?"

"It could have been Jane."

"The day you mistake me for Jane Sandoval is the day I slit my wrists."

"So dramatic," Blair chided. "Where is Jane, by the way?"

"I haven't seen her since Dylan kicked us out of her room. And where is *he*, may I ask?"

"Out," Blair said.

"In this weather?"

"He's walking the grounds," Ava said. "Making sure everything is all right."

"Our hero. I hope he gets back in time for our little Game of Secrets. I doubt he'll want to miss that." Celeste's voice dripped sarcasm. "Too bad Tony isn't here."

If she wanted to get a rise out of Blair, she failed. Blair merely smiled. "Yes, things could get interesting."

"As if they aren't already," Celeste muttered.

"Oh, just you wait."

"Wait for what?" Celeste rose slowly. "If you have something to say to me, Blair, then say it. Don't hide behind some stupid game."

"You sound paranoid."

"As if we don't all have a right to be." Celeste glanced around the room. "These candles bother me."

"I thought you liked the ambience," Blair said, still smiling.

"It's the scent. I can't place it."

"Mandarin and pomegranate," Jane said from the archway. "It was always Lily's favorite."

Celeste grew increasingly agitated. "I might have known you were behind this. Using her scent is creepy as hell, Janie."

Ava was a little creeped out, too. "Maybe the candles weren't such a good idea."

"You replaced the candles?" Blair asked in surprise. "Why?"

Jane shrugged. "Why not? It's like having Lily here with us. She always loved the Game of Secrets. No one played it better. Don't be surprised if she still has something to reveal."

"Jane, stop," Ava said sharply.

"Why? Are you afraid of what she'll say about you? You're not the paragon of virtue you'd have us believe, now are you, Ava?"

Blair's hand crept to her throat as she stared across the room at Jane. "What are you wearing?"

"Don't you like it?" She came into the room and twirled. She had on a white dress identical to the one Lily had worn the night she died. And Jane's hair was different, too. At first, Ava thought she must have bleached it, but then she realized that Jane had donned a wig in either a very cruel or a very sick parody of their dead friend.

She said in shock, "Jane, what do you think you're doing?"

"Call me Lily." She laughed at their gasps and twirled again, arms outstretched, face tilted skyward. It took Ava a moment to realize that Jane was simulating a fall from a very high building.

Ava rushed across the room and grabbed her arms. "Jane, stop it!"

Jane shoved her aside. "You don't get to tell me what to do, Ava. None of you do. You people don't make the rules anymore."

"You're crazy," Celeste said. "You've gone completely off your rocker."

"Then I'm in good company, aren't I?" Jane taunted. She let her gaze travel around the room exactly as she'd done earlier. Only now, her behavior had progressed from petty and resentful to unhinged and diabolical. "I know what you did to her." This to Ava. "I know what all of you did to her. You think she took your secrets to the grave with her, but she didn't. I have them right here in the palm of my hand." She opened her fist, displaying three precisely folded pieces of paper. She glanced up with a smile. "You people have no idea how long I've waited for this night."

Chapter Twelve

Dylan came out of the cabin and stood for a moment, his senses on full alert. He tried his phone again, walking slowly from one end of the porch to the other. Still no signal. Returning the phone to his pocket, he hurried down the steps and headed for the trail. The rain droned on, accompanied now by the rumble of thunder and the crack of lightning over the woods. The storm was getting closer. He needed to get back to the ranch before the weather worsened. Already he felt weighed down by worry and fear and the drag of mud beneath his feet.

He carried his weapon at his side, moving as quickly as he could across the ridge. Twenty feet below, the creek roiled and steamed where the warm underground springs mingled with the cold floodwaters. He lost his footing and in the split second it took to right himself, he saw someone ahead of him on the path. Whoever was there wore a hood pulled over his features. He stood facing Dylan, shoulders hunched against the rain, hands balled into fists at his sides as if he meant to charge.

Dylan braced himself on the slippery trail and steadied his weapon with both hands. "Stay right where you are," he yelled into the storm. "I'm armed."

The figure didn't move. For a moment it seemed as if he were daring Dylan to come after him, but then he turned, left the trail and fled into the woods.

Dylan wiped rainwater from his face and took off after him. He sprinted through the trees, pausing now and then to listen, but the storm drowned out any noise from his quarry. He could be anywhere by now. If he were a local, he'd know the terrain better than Dylan. *Just let him go. Stop wasting time and get back to the house.*

As he turned toward the ridge, he caught a glimpse of something yellow out of the corner of his eye. His weapon came up before he realized he'd spotted a discarded rain slicker.

The poncho had been wadded up and stuffed deep inside a thicket of blackberry vines that had somewhat protected it from the weather.

Dylan tried to fish the slicker out with a stick, but the fabric caught on the brambles. He took another quick check of his surroundings and then hunkered on the ground, reaching deep into the thicket and wincing as thorns jabbed his arms. He caught the slippery fabric between two fingers and as he hauled it out, something fell to the ground with a thud.

Blinded by rain and darkness, he pulled out his phone and angled the beam downward. A tire iron lay on the ground at his feet. Dylan knelt, shining the light along the metal, searching for DNA evidence that would soon be washed away by the rain. Then he refocused the beam inside the thicket. He was so intent on the business at hand he almost missed the signals. The rustle of leaves, the snap of a twig. It wasn't so much that he heard these things as sensed them.

He glanced up. Someone was perched on a low branch staring down at him. Before he could take aim, the figure leaped down upon him. The weight and momentum felled him.

The ground and a knee to his chest knocked the breath from him. Somehow Dylan managed to cling to his weapon and as he brought it up, a hand caught his wrist. A shot went off in the air and then another. And then the gun went flying.

The attacker reached for his throat as Dylan punched hard, clipping the man's chin. Dylan heard a snap and then something warm dripped down on his face. He blinked hard to clear his vision as he drove his fist into the assailant's jaw. They fought in total darkness. Thrashing on the wet ground. Rolling through mud and brambles and splatters of their own blood.

Not once did Dylan get a clear look at his attacker, but he knew from his opponent's size and strength, he was dealing with a male in peak physical condition. Someone around his age. Someone who wasn't afraid to fight dirty. Someone who may have killed Noah Pickett in cold blood with a tire iron.

In a flash of lightning, Dylan spotted his weapon on the ground and lunged for it. Just as his fingers closed around the grip, he was hit hard at the back of the head. Light exploded behind his eyes as a white-hot pain seared his skull.

He collapsed facedown on the ground, not unconscious but too dazed to muster an offense. In some corner of his mind an image formed of that tire iron, dripping with blood. He waited for the kill shot, the blow that would take him out permanently. It never came.

The man got up and Dylan rolled over, trying to get a look at him. He saw nothing but a blurred figure staring down at him.

JANE HAD EXITED the room several minutes ago but the other three stood stone still, too stunned to move or speak, too shocked to even process what had just happened.

Celeste finally broke the silence. "She's lost it. She's gone completely insane. I always knew she had a few screws loose, but I never dreamed she was this far gone."

"She does seem unstable," Blair offered. "I'm not sure what we should do."

"Do? I don't know about the two of you, but I'm getting the hell out of here." Celeste headed for the doorway. "If you think I'm spending one more night under the same roof with that crazy bitch, you've got another think coming."

"And just where will you go?" Ava demanded. "The nearest town is ten miles away and the road is underwater. You can't walk. You can't get a vehicle through. You go out there and the rest of us will just have to come looking for you."

Celeste wasn't fazed. "Then I'll call the cops. Someone should know what we're dealing with here. You know, so that when our bodies are found after the water goes down, they'll know who to look for. Of course, Jane will be long gone by then."

"That's being a little dramatic," Ava said.

"Besides which, you can't call the cops," Blair added. "I tried to get through to Tony a little while ago. There's no signal."

Ava whirled. "*What?* Since when?"

"I don't know. I've tried a few times. The storm must have taken out the tower."

Celeste whipped out her phone. "No service. What about yours, Ava?"

"I broke it in the canyon this morning. Has anyone tried the landline?"

"Nothing but static," Blair said.

The room fell silent as they digested this latest development.

Then Celeste said slowly, "Let me get this straight. We can't leave, we can't call out. We're completely cut off from the outside world." She turned toward the doorway, her gaze lifting to the staircase beyond the foyer. "Do either of you think any of this is coincidental?"

No, it did not seem at all coincidental. Ava tried to keep a cool head, but panic had already gripped her spine. She drew a breath and clung to her composure. "You can't blame Jane for the weather. It's not unusual to lose phone service during a storm, especially with county-wide flooding."

"She's right," Blair said. "The signal out here is iffy in the best of times."

"Let's try to stay calm." Ava spread her hands at her sides as if she could physically tamp down her nerves. "The only thing we can do at the moment is sit tight. We're safer inside than we are out there. I admit, Jane's performance was a little disturbing, but that's all it was. A performance. She's trying to get a rise out of us. I'll go up and talk to her."

Celeste rolled her eyes. "And say what, for crying out loud? Nice dress?"

"I'll let her know that she'd better not pull something like that again."

"Tough talk. Your mistake is thinking that you can reason with her, but whatever. Knock yourself out. You do your thing and I'll do mine." Celeste turned back to the door.

"Where are you going?" Ava called after her.

"Up to my room. Is that allowed?"

"Promise me you won't try to leave."

"Oh, good grief. Just keep that nutjob away from me."

She disappeared through the doorway, and Ava turned back to Blair. "You weren't kidding when you said this could be an interesting evening."

"Not exactly what I had in mind." Blair flattened a hand against her chest. "That dress Jane had on…it couldn't be the same one, could it? Oh, Ava, that's too disturbing to even contemplate."

"It's not the same one. Jane liked to copy Lily's style, remember? She probably bought the same dress."

"And kept it all these years? For *this*?"

"I can't pretend to understand Jane's behavior, but whatever she has in mind, she came prepared." Ava glanced around uneasily. "That dress, the wig, these candles. No wonder she was so insistent that we play the game. Evidently she had the evening all planned out."

Blair was twisting her ring again. "What do you think she wrote on those notes? She said they were Lily's secrets."

Ava shivered. "I don't know."

Blair walked back over to the windows to glance out at the storm. "I wish Tony were here. He'd know what to do."

"You say it's been hours since you were able to get through to him?"

"Yes, why?" Blair's eyes widened in distress. "You don't think something's happened to him, do you?"

"No, of course not. You said yourself, the storm probably took out the cell tower. Let's not think the worst, okay? Maybe we should talk about something else. And come away from that window." Ava sat down on the sofa. "Let's just sit and relax."

Blair took the armchair that Celeste had vacated. "What do you want to talk about?"

"I don't know. Tell me about Whispering Springs. Did you help design the renovations?"

"I had some ideas."

Ava nodded. "I can see your hand here. It's quite a place. I didn't even know that you and Tony owned the ranch until Celeste mentioned it." Ava purposely kept her voice low and conversational, as much to soothe her own anxieties as Blair's. She needed to take her mind off Dylan. Where in the world was he?

"Tony always loved this place. You remember how attached he was back in college. As soon as he heard the property was on the market, he snatched it up. At first, he planned to use it as a personal retreat, a place to come to on weekends and holidays, but then he saw the investment potential and he brought in partners. I offered a few suggestions, but he had a team of architects and designers that did most of the work. Tony never does things in half measures."

"That's probably why he's so successful," Ava said.

"Yes. He conducts a lot of business out here. Some executives like to negotiate on a golf course, but Tony says there's no better way of getting the upper hand than by trapping someone halfway up Bishop's Rock."

"I can see how that would be effective," Ava murmured. "He didn't mind you closing the retreat for our reunion?"

"No. In fact, it was his idea."

Ava lifted a brow. "His idea? Really? A pity he isn't here to enjoy it, then." She paused. "I understand Noah Pickett's family used to own the property. How did he come to work here?"

Blair seemed to have calmed down. She held her hand in front of her as she absently studied her ring. "I don't really know the details. I remember Tony saying something about Noah having gotten out of the service and looking for work. Whispering Springs needed a tour guide and no one knew the area better than Noah. He started working part-time and now he helps runs the place."

"On the drive in from the airport, he told me about a girl who disappeared from here. He said she went for a walk after work and was never heard from again. Her name was Sara, I think."

"Sara Rainey."

"You knew her?" Ava asked.

Blair shrugged. "Not really, although I met most of the employees when the ranch first opened. Tony was devastated when it happened. I'd never seen him so shaken. The retreat had only been open for a few months. The PR was a nightmare. But it wasn't just about the business. That girl was an employee and Tony felt responsible for her. He took her disappearance very personally."

"What did he think happened to her?"

Blair turned her hand to catch candlelight in her diamond. "He never liked to talk about it. He would get very upset whenever her name was mentioned. The only other time I've seen him so upset—" She broke off, as if afraid of revealing more than she meant to.

"Go on."

"Nothing. It doesn't matter."

"Were you about to say after Lily's suicide? I didn't know she and Tony were particularly close."

Blair's chin came up. "Suicide is devastating no matter the circumstances."

"Yes, of course. I didn't mean to imply otherwise."

Blair was silent for a moment. The candlelight playing across her face gave her a sly, mysterious look. "Actually, they were closer than you might think."

Ava tried not to react. "Oh?"

She looked past Ava to the doorway and to the staircase beyond. "I have a feeling that's one of the secrets that Jane had in her hand."

"About Tony?"

"Lily used to have a thing for him. I think they may even have had a little fling at one time."

Ava said in shock, "Why do you think so?"

"Oh, it was just little things I picked up on. Stolen glances. Accidental touches. I noticed it right after she and Dylan broke up. I think Tony was her rebound."

"Did you ask him?"

"No. Why would I?" She shrugged. "Even if they had an affair, it was meaningless. Just sex."

"Did you confront Lily?"

There was a slight hesitation before she said, "Sometimes it's best to let these things run their course."

She talked as if she'd had some experience in dealing with such things. Ava thought about Tony's assignation with Celeste the night before. "I guess that's one way of handling it. I'm not sure I could, though."

Blair smiled. "Maybe that's why you're still single. You aren't prepared to make the necessary sacrifices."

EVERYONE HAD GONE back upstairs and Ava was alone in the great room. Despite her admonishments to Blair, she stood in front of the windows monitoring the storm as she waited for Dylan. When she finally saw him stumble out of the woods, she ran outside to meet him, wrapping an arm around his waist and drawing his arm over her shoulders to support him. His clothing was muddy and bloodstained. She tightened her hold on him and helped him back to the patio.

"Dylan, what happened? My God, all that blood…how badly are you hurt?"

"It's a head wound. Not as bad as it looks." He put a hand to the back of his skull. "Someone ambushed me."

Ava gasped. "The same person you followed into the woods?"

"I don't know for sure. I never got a look at his face."

Ava pulled him underneath the patio lights

so that she could examine the wound. "I can't tell how deep it is. We need to get it cleaned up."

"In a minute. I need to tell you something first." Dylan leaned heavily against the patio wall. "Noah Pickett is dead. Someone killed him."

"What? *How? When?*"

"He's been dead for several hours, maybe since late morning. I found him in one of the cabins."

"My God." Ava pressed back against the wall. "You think the same person who attacked you killed him?"

"I don't know. The cabin had been tossed. I don't think it was a looter. Someone was looking for something."

"This is unbelievable. And I thought things had gotten crazy *here*."

"What do you mean?" Dylan took her arm. "Are you okay?"

"Yes, I'm fine. But it seems like everyone has gone off the deep end. People are acting so strangely, Dylan. But nothing compared to what you've been through. How was Noah murdered?"

"Blows to the head, probably with a tire

iron, and then he was hauled into the hot tub. Cause of death will have to be determined by an autopsy." He glanced inside the French doors. "Where is everyone?"

"Upstairs. There was a scene with Jane. I'll tell you about it later, but we need to take care of that wound first. Dylan—" She moved closer. "We don't have cell service and the landline is dead. I tried to convince the others it was because of the storm, but now I'm worried that someone is deliberately isolating us."

"My phone's dead, too," he said. "It could be the storm or it could be a jammer."

"Most jammers only have the range of a city block," Ava said.

"Not the big ones. Not the ones that are powered by a dedicated generator. They can block the signal for miles."

"That would take a lot of money and a lot of planning, wouldn't it? Maybe Tony's business rivals really are behind this. They'd certainly have the know-how. But I can't see how Noah would fit into that scheme unless he saw something he shouldn't have. And why terrorize the rest of us just to get to Tony Redding?"

"That's what we have to find out," Dylan said.

Ava glanced over her shoulder. "We have to tell the others about Noah. We can't keep it from them."

"I don't know if that's a good idea. Think about it for a minute. We're basically trapped here. The last thing we need is mass panic. We have to keep everyone calm and inside. You said yourself, there's safety in numbers. I'll need your help with that."

"I'll do what I can, but Celeste has already threatened to leave. I'm hoping it was just bluster."

"We'll take care of Celeste if it comes to that, but first things first. I need to get upstairs and get cleaned up before anyone sees me looking like this."

Ava nodded and clung to his hand for a moment before slipping back through the door. When she saw that the coast was clear, she motioned him inside. He went quickly up the stairs, and she grabbed a towel from the guest washroom to clean up his wet footprints. She was glad for the chore. It gave her something to focus on instead of Noah Pickett's murder.

She looked up to find Celeste watching her from the top of the stairs. Her eyes glinted as she cocked her head. "What are you doing,

Ava? Why is your shirt all wet? You didn't go outside, did you? After you ordered the rest of us to stay inside?"

Ava shrugged. "I stepped out on the patio for a minute. The rain blew in harder than I expected. I'm just on my way up to change. Have you seen Blair or Jane?"

Celeste was still staring down at her strangely. "I thought Blair was with you."

"No, she went up a little while ago. At least, I thought she was headed to her room."

Celeste came down the steps slowly. "Has she given up on playing the game? I thought I might join in after all." She opened her hand so that Ava could see a folded note in her palm.

Ava frowned. "There's a bowl in the great room, but are you sure you want to encourage her? Or Jane? Especially Jane," she added with a grimace.

"Maybe they're right. Maybe playing the game is the only way to get to the bottom of what's going on around here."

"You've certainly changed your tune," Ava said suspiciously.

"I'm just trying to adapt to the situation. After Jane's earlier performance, is there any doubt she's behind those creepy dolls? She obviously has something to say, a secret to reveal, and she's using this reunion and the game in particular as her confessional. Who am I to stop her from incriminating herself?"

"Are you that sure she'll incriminate herself?"

"I guess we'll see, won't we? In the meantime, I'm grabbing a bottle of whiskey and locking myself in my room. Call me when the game starts for real."

They passed on the stairs. Ava caught a scent of her perfume, something dark and sultry and cloying. She turned to stare after Celeste. Something about her sudden change in attitude, about her overall demeanor, worried Ava. She seemed a little too confident that Jane would be outed, but for what? Harboring a grudge all these years? Planting mutilated dolls?

Ava watched Celeste disappear into the great room before she turned and hurried up the stairs.

She stopped in her room to change, and then she grabbed the first-aid kit that Blair had left earlier before heading next door to Dylan's room. He let her in wearing nothing but jeans and a grim expression. She followed him into the room and took the nearest chair while he grabbed a shirt from his suitcase and pulled it over his head.

At any other time, the intimacy of the situation might have triggered a response, but cold-blooded murder had a way of suppressing attraction.

"I brought some supplies," she said. "Let me take a look at your head."

"It's fine. I cleaned it in the shower and the bleeding has stopped. We've got more important things to worry about."

She didn't bother arguing. "Dylan, what happened at the cabin? Tell me everything."

He leaned back against the dresser. "The door was open when I got there. I went inside to have a look around. Like I said, the place had been tossed. Drawers pulled out, papers all over the floor. But no Noah. Then I found blood in the bathroom. Not much. Just a few smears on the vanity and backsplash as if someone had tried to clean up in a hurry."

Ava's hand crept to her throat. "Go on."

"I went out to have a look at the creek from the deck. That's when I found him."

"You tried calling the police from the cabin?"

"Yes, of course. That's when I first realized we had a signal problem. I'd made calls earlier in the day, to my office in Houston and to the local authorities to alert them of our situation."

"So they know we're here."

"Yes, but as far as they're concerned, we're not priority. We're on high ground with plenty of supplies and a generator."

Ava sighed. "So the cavalry isn't forthcoming."

His gaze burned into hers. "Ava, we're the cavalry. You and me."

"I wish I found that more comforting. We've only one weapon between us."

"There are other ways to outsmart the enemy, especially now that we know what we're up against. I underestimated the danger. I let my guard down and got myself ambushed, but I won't make that mistake again. We'll be all right. We just need to keep our heads. We've got this, okay?"

"Okay." But Ava couldn't quite quell the tremor in the pit of her stomach. It was one thing to face off against the bad guys in a courtroom, quite another to search for a killer on an isolated ranch. "Did you find anything else at the cabin?"

"Someone had gone through a bunch of newspaper clippings and old photographs of Whispering Springs. The articles were about that girl's disappearance you mentioned. You said Jane had gotten all worked up about it."

"She implied something supernatural had taken the woman. I thought at the time she was just trying to get a rise, but given her earlier behavior, I'm not so sure." Ava paused. "There's a lot I need to tell you about Jane, but I want to hear more about these clippings. I find it strange that Noah would have saved articles about the incident. He implied on the way here from the airport that the disappearance happened before his time."

Dylan folded his arms. "Then he misled you. He knew that woman. I saw a photograph of the two of them together at the top of Bishop's Rock. They appeared to be a couple."

"He said the cops had gone after the boyfriend, but it was just a ploy to take the heat off the ranch. Are you saying Noah was the suspect?"

"I don't think so. We ran background

checks on the staff. Noah joined the military right out of high school. I'll have to check the timeline, but I think he was still deployed overseas when all this happened."

"And then he came back home and got a job here? Why *here*?"

"What are you thinking?"

Ava shook her head. "I'm not sure. We're missing something. I just can't see how all this fits together yet. It's very frustrating."

"Patience," he advised.

"Not my strong suit." She got up and started to pace. "I'm sure you already know that Noah's family once owned Whispering Springs. They fell on hard times, which is how Tony ended up with the place. He was the owner when the girl disappeared."

Dylan left his place at the dresser and walked over to the window to glance out. "Noah mentioned something to me earlier when we were getting ready to go out looking for you. He said he knows this place better than anyone and there are still places to hide that he hasn't yet found." Dylan turned to face her. "You ask why he came back *here*? I think he's been looking for her body all these years."

Ava had a mental image of Noah out combing the property, braving weather and time as he tirelessly searched through caves and canyons for the remains of his murdered sweetheart. His stoicism was poignant and powerful, especially compared to her own inaction. When Dylan had disappeared from her life, she'd simply gone about her business. Never had she felt more cowardly or insignificant.

She walked over now to stand at his side. "Do you think he found her remains? Maybe that's why he was killed."

"It's possible. Especially if he was starting to put everything together."

"Dylan, what if we've gotten this whole thing wrong? What if none of this has anything to do with Lily? Or us? Or even a business merger? It's always been about that missing girl. Everything that's happened—the dolls, the messages, even the threatening phone calls—has been nothing but misdirection. A clever way for the killer to obscure his true motive."

Dylan glanced at her. "*His* motive?"

"You were attacked by a man, correct?

Think about it," she said. "The one person that's been absent from the start."

"Tony Redding."

Ava searched his profile. "I can tell by your reaction that you've already come to the same conclusion."

He shrugged. "Whoever attacked me was in good shape. About my size and weight. And he knew the property. He knew the trails."

"And you never got a good look at his face. I mean, it's pure speculation, but what if he had an affair with that girl and she threatened to tell Blair? That was early in their marriage when she really did control all the money. Fast-forward to present day and Noah somehow puts it all together. Besides you, who else in our group would have the means and know-how to set up a long-range jammer?"

"It's not that difficult."

Ava paused thoughtfully. "What I don't understand is why he left you alive."

"I don't know. What I do know is that we still need to search these rooms. Which means we need everyone downstairs—"

He broke off as thunder boomed overhead and the lamps flickered. Then the lights went out altogether. Ava pulled her sweater around her and waited in the dark.

"Shouldn't the generator have kicked on by now?"

Dylan moved back into the room. A second later, a flashlight came on. "Something's wrong. I need to go out and have a look."

"Then I'll come with you."

"Ava—"

A muffled scream cut him off. They both tensed in shock, and then Ava clutched his arm. "That came from downstairs."

He tucked her arm through his and pulled her to his side. "Stay close," he whispered.

"Don't worry," she whispered back.

Chapter Thirteen

Dylan eased the door open, and Ava followed him out into the hallway. He moved down the corridor in a slight crouch, flashlight in his left hand, weapon in his right. Odd that no one else came out, she thought as they headed for the staircase. Shadows danced on the walls, making her pulse race.

They were at the top of the stairs when another scream sounded from the great room. They eased down the steps and paused at the doorway before entering. Heart pounding, Ava tracked the flashlight beam over furniture and into all the dark corners. Dylan swept the light from side to side and then jerked the beam back to the fireplace, catching Blair's pale face. She knelt on the floor in front of the hearth. The sight of her was so surprising that it took Ava a moment to register the bloody knife in her hand.

Dylan said sharply, "Place the knife on the floor and put your hands in the air."

Blair just stared at him.

Ava came around him. "Blair, put down the knife."

"Knife? I don't…" She turned and gasped, then scooted away, revealing a body on the floor behind her.

Dylan moved in. "It's Celeste."

That seemed to snap Blair out of her trance. "I didn't do it. You have to believe me. I found her like this."

"Then put the knife down and let's talk about it," Dylan said.

She placed the knife on the floor at his feet. He kicked it aside and then handed Ava the flashlight. She tried to hold the beam steady as he checked for a pulse. There was so much blood. All over Blair's shirt. All over her hands.

And Celeste so pale and still…

"Is she—"

"There's a pulse," Dylan said. "Here, take this." He handed Ava his weapon. "We need to get her someplace safe."

"Should we move her?"

"I'll feel a lot better if we get her behind a locked door," Dylan said. "This room is too exposed. Let's take her upstairs and then we'll worry about the bleeding."

Ava stood back as he lifted Celeste from the floor and started for the stairs. "Don't touch the knife," he warned. "Find something to wrap it in and bring it with you. Bring Blair upstairs, too."

Tucking the gun in her waistband, Ava grabbed a throw from the sofa. As she bent to pick up the knife, the flashlight sparked off the crystal bowl that Blair had set out earlier. There was a folded note inside. A secret.

"Dylan."

He was already halfway across the room with Celeste. "What is it?"

"Someone left a note. Someone is playing the game."

"We already knew that," he said as he headed for the stairs.

Ava wrapped the knife in the wool throw and slid the note in her jeans pocket. Then she grabbed Blair's arm. "Come on. We can't leave you down here. You have to come with us."

"I didn't do it, Ava. I was on the stairs

when the lights went out. I heard her scream and when I came in, I saw a silhouette on the patio. And then I spotted Celeste on the floor…"

"Just come. We'll sort it out upstairs."

She ushered Blair out of the room and they caught up with Dylan at the top of the stairs.

"Put her in my room." Ava brushed past Dylan to unlock the door, then lit his way with the flashlight.

Blair came in with them, hovering at the foot of the bed while Dylan settled Celeste on top of the covers. "Grab towels," he said.

Ava set the flashlight and throw on the nightstand and hurried into the bathroom. She grabbed an armful of towels and came back to the bed. Dylan folded one and pressed it against the leaking wound in Celeste's side. "Keep pressure on it."

Ava changed places with him. "Where are you going?"

"I'll see Blair to her room and then I need to find Jane."

"What about the generator?"

"I'll check on that, too." He nodded toward the bed. "You okay to handle this?"

"Yes, I'm fine."

Blair pressed herself into the wall. "Don't make me leave. Please. I don't want to be alone."

"You'll be fine in your room," Dylan said firmly. "Lock the door and don't let anyone in."

Ava glanced up at him. "Are you sure that's a good idea? Maybe it's best if we stay together."

He leaned in so that only she could hear him. "I don't want her in here with you, understand?"

Her heart jolted. "Yes."

He straightened. "I'll lock the door on my way out. What I just told Blair goes for you, too. Don't let anyone in. Not Blair. Not Jane. Not anyone."

"I won't."

"You have my gun. If anyone tries to force their way in, shoot them. Don't hesitate."

She nodded and turned back to the task at hand.

JANE DIDN'T ANSWER his knock. Dylan called to her through the door, but she still didn't come. He moved along the hallway, down the stairs and crept through the house using his phone for illumination. Grabbing a knife from the kitchen, he let himself out the back door. The rain was still coming down hard and the wind had picked up, buffeting the cold drops against his face as he hurried down the path toward the storage building. In a flash of lightning, he saw someone leaning over the generator.

"Hey!"

The man whipped around and Dylan finally saw his face.

"Stay right where you are, Dylan!"

"I can't do that, Tony!" He started toward him on the path. "Put your hands where I can see them and move away from the generator."

Tony faced him. "You don't know what you're up against. You don't know the whole story."

"Seems pretty obvious you're trying to sabotage the generator."

"I'm trying to fix it! Someone damaged it, but it wasn't me."

Dylan wiped the rain from his face. "Then who?"

"I don't have time to explain. Just let me get the power back on before someone gets hurt."

"Someone's already been hurt. Noah Pickett is dead. But then, you already know that, don't you?"

"I didn't kill him. I found his body just like you did."

"Then why did you run? Why did you attack me?"

"Because I thought you might be working for *her*. It wouldn't be the first time she hired someone to come after me."

"What are you talking about?"

Lightning flickered across Tony's face. "You don't get it, do you? You still don't get it. Why am I the only one who can see her for what she really is? She's a psychopath, Dylan. A killer. She has to be put down."

Dylan's grip tightened on the knife. "Just take it easy."

Lightning glinted off the gun in Tony's hand. "Stand aside, Dylan. Or I'll put you down, too."

AVA LOST TRACK of the time. She had gone through half a dozen towels before the bleeding finally subsided. Celeste's pulse was stronger now and her breathing seemed easier. Ava placed a fresh towel against the wound and rose to work the kinks out of her muscles.

The storm had strengthened in the last few minutes. Thunder shook the walls and rattled the windows. She went over to watch the fireworks for a moment, scouring the sky and the grounds and wondering where Dylan was.

She peered so intently into the night that when a lightning strike revealed a face, she thought for a moment that someone stood on the balcony staring in at her. She gasped and put a hand on the glass. The face smiled.

"Read the secret," a voice said behind her. "Read it aloud, Ava, so that you'll finally know the truth."

Ava whirled. "Celeste…what are you doing? You can't be up—" Her hand went to her waistband. She had placed Dylan's gun on the nightstand.

Celeste lifted the weapon with one hand as she held her side with the other. "It's not life-threatening. No organ damage. I made sure of that. Just enough for a lot of blood."

Ava stared at her in shock. "Why would you do that?"

"Because it's the perfect alibi."

"Alibi…"

The gun came back up. "I said read the secret! It's still in your pocket, isn't it? Read it, Ava. Now!"

Ava cast frantically about for a weapon as she slid her hand in her pocket and withdrew the folded secret.

"Now read it."

"I can't see. It's too dark in here. Let me get the flashlight."

Celeste moved around the room, keeping the gun trained on Ava. She nodded toward the nightstand where Ava had propped Dylan's flashlight. "Go on."

Ava picked up the flashlight, testing the weight as she focused the beam on the note. She stared down at the words and then glanced up.

"Aloud!"

"'Lily didn't jump. I pushed her.'"

Celeste smiled in satisfaction. "Jane was right, you know. Lily still has secrets to share."

The paper floated to the floor from Ava's fingers. "You killed her? *Why?*"

"She had to be taught a lesson. You don't take what doesn't belong to you."

"What did she take?" Ava's voice was barely a whisper. Her whole body trembled but she tried to stay focused as she gripped the rubber flashlight. It wouldn't be much of a weapon, but the knife was still on the nightstand…if she could unwrap the throw…

Celeste's eyes gleamed as lightning flashed. "Tony loves *me*. It's always been me. Not Lily, not Blair, not that stupid little girl who worked here. She thought she could lure him away by following him around, acting all moony and starry-eyed. As if he would ever look at someone like her twice."

Ava placed her hand on the nightstand. "I don't understand any of this."

"Of course you don't. You've never had anyone love you the way Tony loves me. Lily thought she could break our bond by telling Blair about us. I couldn't let that happen. I couldn't let her reveal our secret. The secret is everything. The glue that holds us together. It's what makes our love so strong."

Ava inched her hand toward the throw. "But he's with Blair."

"Because he *has* to be. He has to protect our secret. Everything was fine until Blair decided to have a baby. A kid would ruin everything. Trap him forever. I couldn't let that happen."

"So you came to the reunion to kill her? The dolls, the threatening phone calls, the break-in? You did all that?"

"I had to protect our secret."

"And Noah? He discovered your secret?"

"Seven years," she said in awe. "Seven years and no one ever suspected a thing. And then I come here and he recognizes me. He said he remembered seeing me with Sara. At first he just wanted to ask questions about her, and then he got pushy. He said he had a photograph. He could prove I was here on the day that bitch disappeared."

Someone pounded on the door. "Ava, it's Dylan! Let me in!"

In the split second that Celeste's attention was diverted, Ava jerked the throw off the nightstand. The knife hit the floor and she grabbed it. Then lunged.

The momentum knocked Celeste against the French doors, and the two women sprawled onto the balcony. The force split the railing and they crashed through. For a moment, Ava felt herself in a free fall. Somehow she managed to grab onto the splintered support, but she heard Celeste hit the ground with a thud.

Dylan kicked the door in and rushed onto the balcony. He grabbed Ava's arms and hauled her up, holding her tight for a moment before he grabbed the flashlight and leaped from the balcony in pursuit.

Ava took a moment to catch her breath and then, squeezing her eyes closed, she lowered herself over the balcony and dropped to the ground.

RAIN PEPPERED DYLAN'S FACE. Even with the flashlight, he could barely see the trail in front of him, let alone catch a glimpse of Celeste, but it didn't matter. He knew where she was going. Like a wounded animal, she was headed to the one place where she felt safe, protected. Bishop's Rock.

By the time he got to the base, she'd already scrambled up to a ledge. She fired off a couple of rounds and a ricochet clipped his arm before he could take cover. The next shelf was twenty feet above her. She moved up the wall with terrifying speed, instinctively finding hand-and toeholds in the dark. Dylan angled the beam up the wall, and she froze for a moment like a deer caught in headlights. She hung by one hand as she fired at him again. Then she tucked the gun away and went up another ten feet. Dylan followed her up.

"There's nowhere to go, Celeste!" he called through the storm. "It's over. Tony told me everything."

"He told you what he needed to! He's protecting our secret!"

"There is no secret, Celeste! Tony loves Blair! You have to accept that. You have to leave them alone. Come down so we can get you to a hospital."

"I'm not coming down! Tony told me to wait for him at the top!"

"Tony's back at the house with Blair. Come down and let's end this before anyone else gets hurt!"

He was close enough now that he could see her without the light. She was flat against the wall, hanging with both hands as she tried to swing herself over to the ledge. Her fingers slipped and she dropped, managing to grab the edge of the rock, but she was too weak to pull herself up.

Dylan went up after her. "Hang on, Celeste. I'm almost there."

She gazed down at him. "I didn't want to kill Lily. She was my friend and I loved her. But she was going to tell. She was going to ruin everything."

"I know. Just hang on."

"I can't live without Tony."

"Celeste—"

She pushed off with her hands, spreading her arms wide as she fell backward.

AVA WAS HALFWAY UP to Dylan when he spotted her in the rain. He scrambled down to a ledge and pulled her beside him. They huddled together beneath an overhang.

"What do you think you're doing?" he asked tenderly. "You're terrified of heights."

"I know, but I heard shots. I was more terrified that you'd been hit—"

"So you thought you'd come up and rescue me?"

"Obviously I didn't think. I just climbed."

He pulled her to him. "Celeste is dead."

"I know. I saw her fall. Dylan, what happened? She kept telling me how much Tony loved her, but I don't really understand any of this."

"It's a long story. I'll tell you what I know of it, but first we have to get you down."

"No." She placed her hands on his cheeks. "First you have to kiss me."

Chapter Fourteen

"It started back in college," Tony said. "I knew her behavior was strange, obsessive. No one else could see it. She acted normal around you all. Like a different person. I was flattered by the attention at first, but then she killed Lily and everything changed. My life hasn't been the same since."

"Why didn't you go to the police?" Ava asked.

He looked at her defiantly. "You think I didn't want to? She threatened to hurt Blair. After what she'd done to Lily, I couldn't take that chance."

"I always knew she was crazy," Jane said. "She slipped something in my drink once and almost caused me to wreck my car. I think she did the same thing to Lily. That's why she was acting so erratically before she died."

They were all seated around the great room. Tony and Blair were huddled together on the sofa, Jane had taken an armchair and Dylan leaned against the wall, arms folded as he stared out the window watching the storm. Ava perched on the hearth, watching Dylan watch the storm.

Even as she listened to the explanations, she wondered how long it would be before they could be alone. So much had happened and there was still so much to say. So many secrets to share…

She shivered and tried to focus on the conversation.

"Blair was her leverage," Tony explained. "She knew that I would do anything to protect her. And as long as she could pretend to be Blair's friend, she had a connection to me." He squeezed his wife's hand. "You have no idea what it's been like. The trouble she's caused for me personally and for my businesses. She was convinced that I was in love with her and everything I said and did to get rid of her was just to protect our secret. There's a name for her affliction. Erotomania. Sometimes she'd move on to someone else. There would be long periods of calm and then she'd turn up again, ingratiating herself into Blair's life. When she found out we were trying to get pregnant, things got worse. She threatened to kill Blair. I knew I had to do something then. The police couldn't stop her and so I had to."

"That's why you suggested Whispering Springs for the reunion," Ava said. "It's remote and you know the terrain."

"You mistook Ava for her in the canyon," Dylan said. He didn't look at all impressed with Tony's revelations.

"I told her to meet me on the trail at the bottom and then I pretended to leave." Tony turned to Ava. "I'm sorry. I never meant to hurt you."

"I can see how you'd be at your wit's end," she said. "I've prosecuted stalkers. I know how devious and persistent they can be, but there isn't much you can do legally until a line is crossed. By then, it's too late."

"I'm just glad it's over and done with," Jane said. "And now Lily finally has justice."

"In no small part thanks to you," Ava said.

"That was quite a performance earlier. I think it may have tipped Celeste over the edge."

"I didn't mean for her to snap. I just wanted her to admit what she'd done."

"Mission accomplished."

"The storm's moving on," Dylan said.

They all got up and went over to the windows.

He checked his phone. "Still no service."

"You don't need to worry about me," Tony said. "When the roads clear, I'll turn myself in." He hugged Blair close. "No more secrets."

A LITTLE WHILE LATER, Ava joined Dylan on the patio. "What a night. I'm exhausted and yet wired at the same time."

He propped a hand on a post. "I know what you mean. I don't feel the least bit sleepy."

"How's the arm? And the head? God, all these injuries. We're quite a pair."

He met her gaze in the dark. "I agree."

She shivered as she stepped up to the railing and searched the sky. "I see a few stars twinkling out. It really is over, isn't it?"

"It's as over as you want it to be, Ava."

She turned to face him. "It's up to me, then?"

He slid his fingers through her hair. "I'll call you when we get back to the city."

"You'd better."

He smiled, making her pulse race. "It's late. We should probably try to get some sleep."

"My room or yours?"

"As easy as that, huh?"

"As easy as that." She pulled him to her. "I let you go once, Dylan. I'm hanging on for dear life this time."

"You'd better," he said against her lips.

* * * * *

Looking for more Amanda Stevens?
Check out

PINE LAKE

available now from Harlequin Intrigue!

Get 2 Free Books,
Plus 2 Free Gifts—
just for trying the Reader Service!

HARLEQUIN *Presents*

YES! Please send me 2 FREE Harlequin Presents® novels and my 2 FREE gifts (gifts are worth about $10 retail). After receiving them, if I don't wish to receive any more books, I can return the shipping statement marked "cancel." If I don't cancel, I will receive 6 brand-new novels every month and be billed just $4.55 each for the regular-print edition or $5.55 each for the larger-print edition in the U.S., or $5.49 each for the regular-print edition or $5.99 each for the larger-print edition in Canada. That's a saving of at least 11% off the cover price! It's quite a bargain! Shipping and handling is just 50¢ per book in the U.S. and 75¢ per book in Canada*. I understand that accepting the 2 free books and gifts places me under no obligation to buy anything. I can always return a shipment and cancel at any time. The free books and gifts are mine to keep no matter what I decide.

Please check one: ☐ Harlequin Presents® Regular-Print ☐ Harlequin Presents® Larger-Print
 (106/306 HDN GMWK)   (176/376 HDN GMWK)

Name _____ (PLEASE PRINT) _____

Address _____ Apt. # _____

City _____ State/Prov. _____ Zip/Postal Code _____

Signature (if under 18, a parent or guardian must sign)

Mail to the Reader Service:
IN U.S.A.: P.O. Box 1341, Buffalo, NY 14240-8531
IN CANADA: P.O. Box 603, Fort Erie, Ontario L2A 5X3

Want to try two free books from another series?
Call 1-800-873-8635 or visit www.ReaderService.com.

* Terms and prices subject to change without notice. Prices do not include applicable taxes. Sales tax applicable in N.Y. Canadian residents will be charged applicable taxes. Offer not valid in Quebec. This offer is limited to one order per household. Books received may not be as shown. Not valid for current subscribers to Harlequin Presents books. All orders subject to approval. Credit or debit balances in a customer's account(s) may be offset by any other outstanding balance owed by or to the customer. Please allow 4 to 6 weeks for delivery. Offer available while quantities last.

Your Privacy—The Reader Service is committed to protecting your privacy. Our Privacy Policy is available online at www.ReaderService.com or upon request from the Reader Service.

We make a portion of our mailing list available to reputable third parties that offer products we believe may interest you. If you prefer that we not exchange your name with third parties, or if you wish to clarify or modify your communication preferences, please visit us at www.ReaderService.com/consumerschoice or write to us at Reader Service Preference Service, P.O. Box 9062, Buffalo, NY 14240-9062. Include your complete name and address.

HPI7R3

Get 2 Free Books,
Plus 2 Free Gifts—
just for trying the Reader Service!

YES! Please send me 2 FREE Harlequin® Romance Larger-Print novels and my 2 FREE gifts (gifts are worth about $10 retail). After receiving them, if I don't wish to receive any more books, I can return the shipping statement marked "cancel." If I don't cancel, I will receive 4 brand-new novels every month and be billed just $5.34 per book in the U.S. or $5.74 per book in Canada. That's a savings of at least 15% off the cover price! It's quite a bargain! Shipping and handling is just 50¢ per book in the U.S. and 75¢ per book in Canada*. I understand that accepting the 2 free books and gifts places me under no obligation to buy anything. I can always return a shipment and cancel at any time. The free books and gifts are mine to keep no matter what I decide.

119/319 HDN GMWL

Name _____ (PLEASE PRINT) _____

Address _____ Apt. #

City _____ State/Prov. _____ Zip/Postal Code

Signature (if under 18, a parent or guardian must sign) _____

Mail to the **Reader Service:**

IN U.S.A.: P.O. Box 1341, Buffalo, NY 14240-8531
IN CANADA: P.O. Box 603, Fort Erie, Ontario L2A 5X3
Want to try two free books from another line?
Call 1-800-873-8635 or visit www.ReaderService.com.

*Terms and prices subject to change without notice. Prices do not include applicable taxes. Sales tax applicable in N.Y. Canadian residents will be charged applicable taxes. Offer not valid in Quebec. This offer is limited to one order per household. Books received may not be as shown. Not valid for current subscribers to Harlequin Romance Larger-Print books. All orders subject to approval. Credit or debit balances in a customer's account(s) may be offset by any other outstanding balance owed by or to the customer. Please allow 4 to 6 weeks for delivery. Offer available while quantities last.

Your Privacy—The Reader Service is committed to protecting your privacy. Our Privacy Policy is available online at www.ReaderService.com or upon request from the Reader Service.

We make a portion of our mailing list available to reputable third parties that offer products we believe may interest you. If you prefer that we not exchange your name with third parties, or if you wish to clarify or modify your communication preferences, please visit us at www.ReaderService.com/consumerschoice or write to us at Reader Service Preference Service, P.O. Box 9062, Buffalo, NY 14240-9062. Include your complete name and address.

READERSERVICE.COM

Manage your account online!

- Review your order history
- Manage your payments
- Update your address

We've designed the
Reader Service website
just for you.

Enjoy all the features!

- Discover new series available to you, and read excerpts from any series.
- Respond to mailings and special monthly offers.
- Browse the Bonus Bucks catalog and online-only exculsives.
- Share your feedback.

Visit us at:
ReaderService.com